W9-AKY-389

Pearl's Promise

Pearl's Promise

Written and illustrated by

FRANK ASCH

DELACORTE PRESS / NEW YORK

To Peg, John, Linda, Patty, and Leigh

Published by
Delacorte Press
1 Dag Hammarskjold Plaza
New York, N.Y. 10017

Manufactured in the United States of America

First printing

Designed by Judith Neuman

Library of Congress Cataloging in Publication Data

Asch, Frank.
Pearl's promise.

Summary: With her brother in the clutches of a python in a pet shop, Pearl, a white mouse, goes through hair-raising adventures to rescue him.
[1. Mice—Fiction] I. Title.
PZ7.A778Pe 1984 [E] 83-17153
ISBN 0-385-29325-9
ISBN 0-385-29321-6 (lib. bdg.)

Pearl's Promise

(1)

I'll never forget the day Momma and Poppa were sold. It was a hot August afternoon, and business in Adams's Pet Store was slow as usual. Mr. Adams was sitting in front of a fan mopping his forehead with a handkerchief and watching TV. Most of us in the cage were watching too.

When a commercial came on, my momma said to me:

"Pearl, save my place." And she got up to get a drink of water.

Just then a skinny kid with thick eyeglasses came into the store. The next thing we knew, Mr. Adams was opening the cage door and he had Momma by the tail. She squirmed to get loose, but his grasp was too firm.

"Be good children!" Momma called to us. "And take good care of little Tony."

Poppa was taking a nap at the time. When he heard Momma's call, he woke up with a start.

"Fight back!" he screamed. But it was too late.

As Momma tried to swing around and bite Mr. Adams, he let go, and she fell into a tall white cardboard box.

Poppa was crushed. He rubbed his eyes as if he couldn't believe what he had just seen. Then he staggered a few steps and collapsed into a heap.

But the skinny kid with the thick eyeglasses wanted two mice. As soon as Mr. Adams opened the cage door everyone ran to the opposite side of the cage. Everyone, that is, but Poppa. He crouched bravely by the door with his tail straight in the air.

"I'm sorry, children," he called to us. "But I simply must go with your momma."

Albert, my older brother, ran up to him.

"Poppa!" he cried. "Don't leave us!"

There were tears in Poppa's eyes as Mr. Adams took him from our cage and dropped him into the tall white cardboard box. It was the last we ever saw of them.

That night we went off in a corner by ourselves and talked about it.

"Momma never did like it in this cage," Albert muttered woefully.

"Yeah. Maybe she'll be happier now," I said.

"And Poppa will be too," said my little brother Tony.

"How do you figure that?" asked Albert.

"Because now I can't pester him to tell me stories all the time," said Tony.

"Poppa liked to tell you stories," I said. "That was one of his favorite things."

"But who will tell me stories now?" sobbed Tony.

We all felt so alone. Without saying anything, we huddled together into a tight circle.

"We'll both tell you stories," said Albert.

Momma and Poppa taught Albert and me a lot about pet-store life, but Tony was much younger than we were and still had a lot to learn. At first Albert tried to teach him, but Albert was a lousy teacher; no patience at all. He always ended up screaming at Tony and making him feel stupid. Besides, what Albert really wanted to do was practice his writing.

It was an obsession with him. Several of us had learned how to read from watching TV, but that wasn't enough for Albert. He wanted to learn how to write. Hour after hour he toiled by the water bottle getting his tail wet and tracing out letters on the metal bottom of our cage.

As he withdrew ever more into himself and his work, I had to take over and teach Tony everything. We started out on the exercise wheel. The important thing about that is learning how to get on and off without getting your tail pinched or getting thrown into the food dish. Then I taught him the basic points of etiquette, like how to drink from the water bottle so the cedar shavings beneath stay dry and how to sleep in a huddle on cold winter nights without getting stepped on. Tony was an intelligent mouse, but he was so unsure of himself, I had to go over everything a

AFTER ALL, YOU'RE NOT MOMMA'S LITTLE BABY ANYMORE!

hundred times before he was convinced that he really did know it.

Sometimes he just wouldn't pay attention. Again and again I told him:

"You've got to learn to take care of yourself. After all, you're not Momma's little baby anymore!"

Taking care of Tony kept me busy, but there were times when I couldn't help feeling left behind. I missed Momma and Poppa so much. Sometimes in the middle of the night, I'd wake up and forget they were gone. I'd look around for them and call out their names. Then I'd remember and feel sad.

Nothing seemed worthwhile anymore. I didn't want to work out on the exercise wheel or even watch television. Sometimes late in the afternoon I'd get to feeling so lonely, I'd just crawl down under the cedar shavings and cry myself to sleep.

Then one dismal day I heard someone else down there crying with me. I edged a little closer and poked through the cedar shavings. At first I couldn't see very much, just the tip of an ear and a whisker or two. When I brushed away some of the shavings I saw a large mouse with a long nose and a short tail.

"Go away!" he whined. "Leave me alone!"

As soon as he spoke I recognized his raspy voice and remembered his name: Wilbur. He seemed very embarrassed, so I was going to leave, but something made me stay.

"If it makes you feel any better," I said, "I was just crying too."

Wilbur heaved a big sigh and brushed away some of the cedar shavings that remained between us.

"Why were you crying?" he asked with a sniffle.

At first I tried to hedge. "Oh, no reason," I said.

But slowly he drew me out and got the whole story. I ended up pouring out my heart to him, telling him all about Momma and Poppa, and Albert and Tony too. While I talked he just listened. He didn't snicker or say things that made me feel silly. When I was done, I felt all emptied out inside, like a freshly washed fish tank.

"Did you see the kid who bought my parents?" asked Wilbur. "He looked like the budding young scientist type. I wouldn't be surprised if he chopped off their tails just to see if they would grow back!"

"Your parents were bought too?"

"Yeah," said Wilbur, "so I know how you feel." Then he paused to scratch his ear. "I never told anyone this before, but sometimes I go off by myself and talk to them. I tell them all kinds of things and pretend they can really hear me. It makes me feel a little better. . . . Yeah, I really miss them a whole lot. But that's not why I was crying today."

There was a long pause. I didn't know what to say, so I just kept quiet.

"Today some of the other mice ganged up on me and pushed me off the exercise wheel," Wilbur blurted out as a large tear welled up in his eye. "I fell right on my face and they just laughed!"

"I know the mice you're talking about." I tried to

console him. "And you shouldn't pay them any mind. They just watch so much mean stuff on TV, after a while it makes them mean."

"Sometimes I wish I could be just like them," sobbed Wilbur.

"But I like you just the way you are," I said, surprising myself, because usually I'm quite shy. I guess I sensed something different about Wilbur—a caring in him that made him special.

Wilbur wiped the tear from the side of his nose with the tip of his tail. Then he smiled as yet another tear rolled down the side of his cheek.

Having someone like Wilbur to talk to made a big difference. I still felt sad about Momma and Poppa, but at least now I didn't have to feel so lonely. In fact, in the days and weeks that followed, Wilbur and I became best all-time forever friends! We talked and talked, made up games, and played together all day long.

Tony liked Wilbur too. Once when Tony stayed up watching monster movies and woke up with nightmares, Wilbur was the only one who could get him back to sleep.

There were so many scary programs on TV, and Mr. Adams watched them all. The first thing he did every morning was make himself a cup of coffee and turn on the TV. He kept it on all day long, watching whatever came on—quiz shows, soap operas, sit-coms, wrestling, news—you name it, he watched it. Bleary-eyed, he watched TV late into the night until the stations went off the air, and there was nothing but fuzzy dots on the screen. He watched the fuzzy dots for a while and then he went to bed.

There were cobwebs on the ceiling, his parakeets caught cold, his puppies turned mean, and there were always a few fish floating upside down in his fish tanks. He didn't take very good care of himself either. He wore the same old gray sweater and baggy overalls every day. I doubt that he washed them twice a month. He always needed a shave, and what little hair he had left on his head went without combing.

Wilbur and I liked TV, too, but not that much. Mostly we enjoyed old movies and animal shows. Our favorite was a show called *Forest Friends*. Everyone in the pet store liked that program, even the turtles.

Every week *Forest Friends* features a different animal. My favorite was the one about ants. Did you know that some ants keep tiny bugs called aphids and milk them just like cows?

One week the whole show was about snakes. Snakes are very interesting creatures. They can have as many as three hundred bones in their body. They look slimy like worms but they're not; they're covered with a scaly skin that they shed several times a year. It's called molting.

We were all enjoying the program until the narrator said: "Snakes are often portrayed in movies and literature as evil characters, but only eight in one hundred snakes are poisonous and many are helpful to man in keeping down mice and rat populations."

"Keeping down what?" asked Tony.

"Shhh!" said Albert.

First the narrator showed the snake's special jaws.

"His sharp needlelike teeth are not good for chewing," he said. "But they curve toward the throat, and his jaws unhinge so his mouth can open up very wide for swallowing."

Then right before our eyes they showed how snakes in captivity are fed. They put a mouse into a snake's tank. The snake struck so fast, all you could see was a blur. He coiled himself around the mouse's body. Then he squeezed until the mouse was dead. The poor fellow never had a chance.

Of course, we were all horrified: Albert planned to write a letter of complaint, Wilbur insisted we all take a vow never to watch *Forest Friends* again, and Tony had nightmares for a week! But as Poppa always said, "Mice have long tails and short memories." The following week *Forest Friends* had an hour-long special on elephants. We all watched it and soon forgot all about snakes.

(2)

WILBUR'S SISTER LUCY IS VERY PRETTY. SHE HAS DAINTY paws and very soft fur. But she's not at all like Wilbur. All day long she watches TV just like Mr. Adams. Her favorite thing to watch is commercials, especially perfume commercials. I guess we're all pretty sensitive about smell. When a little kid drags his mother over to our cage and says, "I wanna mouse," more often than not she'll reply, "No, dear. They smell." And it's just not true! Our cages do have to be cleaned regularly, but if that's done, we hardly smell at all. Anyway Lucy has a hang-up about perfume. She loves it: Whenever people come into the store with the least little bit of cologne behind their ears, she takes in huge inhalations and swoons. Sometimes she quotes the latest perfume commercials. Her favorite is "Ahhh . . . it's just like spring!" It's really disgusting! Sometimes I think her one ambition in life, although she says she wants to be a movie star, is to have some little girl buy her and give her all kinds of perfume.

But for all that, she's still not a bad sort of mouse. Sometimes she even condescends to play games with us.

One fall afternoon we were all playing a game Wilbur and I invented called Guess What? The object of the game is to try to guess what each customer is going to buy. We had been playing for some time when a man in a dark blue suit and slicked down hair came into the store. Wilbur guessed that he wanted to buy a choke collar but I said:

"I don't think he wants to buy anything. Look at that briefcase he's got. I say he's a salesman. What do you think, Lucy?"

"Oh, I don't want to play anymore," replied Lucy. "*Dying for Dollars* is coming on soon."

Dying for Dollars is Mr. Adams's favorite quiz show. Lucy likes it because they always give the losing contestants a bottle of perfume as a consolation prize.

"Good afternoon, Mr. Adams," said the man in the dark blue suit. "I'm from Pete's Pets, the total pet care company."

"You win again," said Wilbur. "C'mon. Let's play a few rounds of Hide and Sniff."

"No, wait!" I said. "Let's see if this guy can sell Mr. Adams anything."

The salesman looked carefully around the pet shop. It was probably the messiest store he had ever been in.

DID YOU HEAR THAT?
YIKES!

You could tell he didn't approve, but he never said anything about it to Mr. Adams.

"I've got some interesting new items for you to look at," he said. "For example, we have a new kind of fish food that makes goldfish live twice as long."

"They live too long already!" barked Mr. Adams, who didn't appreciate the interruption.

"Well, then how about a snake? I notice you don't have one."

"Did you hear that?" I gasped.

"Yikes!" said Wilbur.

"What? Another animal in this store?" complained Mr. Adams. "That's the last thing I need!"

The salesman looked over at our cage.

"I see you have an overcrowded mouse cage. A snake would certainly take care of that problem."

"And who's going to take care of the snake?" asked Mr. Adams sarcastically. "The guinea pigs?"

The salesman chuckled. "Well, actually they practically take care of themselves. They only need to be fed twice a month. They're a very clean, low-maintenance item."

Just then the commercial ended and the quiz show returned. Bright lights flashed, and the quiz-show host burst out of a big clock, smiling and tossing fake money in the air.

Tactfully the salesman pretended to be interested in the show. He laughed at the host's silly jokes and attempted to answer the questions before the contestants.

In a few minutes, when another commercial came on, Mr. Adams was in a much better mood.

"Now, about the snake . . ." continued the salesman, leafing through a catalog of glossy full-color photos. "We're overstocked on this reticulated python. You could get him for half price."

"No, don't do it!" screamed Wilbur.

"You'll never sell it!" I squeaked.

"And what if it doesn't sell?" Mr. Adams scratched his head.

"We take it back, no charge," said the salesman.

Mr. Adams was right. The last thing he needed was another animal in the store. But he just couldn't pass up a bargain.

"Okay," he said. "I'll take it."

Wilbur and I looked around. No one else seemed to realize what had just happened. They were all busy doing things on their own or watching *Dying for Dollars*.

We ran over to the water bottle, where Albert was practicing his letters.

"Guess what?" I said. "Mr. Adams is getting a snake!"

"No," said Albert, "he wouldn't do that."

"Oh, yes, he would!" said Wilbur.

"A reticulated python!"

"Oh, come on. You guys are playing a trick on me, aren't you?" said Albert.

"I tell you, he ordered a snake," I said. "He bought one for half price."

I hadn't realized it, but Tony wasn't far away.

"AAHHH! A snake!" he cried.

The bad news spread through the cage faster than fin algae in a tank full of sick guppies. The young ones, like Tony, were overwhelmed and burst out crying. The elders remained somewhat philosophic.

"Well, we all gotta go sometime," they said.

Others were cynical and said things like, "At least pretty soon it won't be so crowded in here."

A few proclaimed that it was retribution for our evil ways.

"It's all that television watching!" they insisted. "The news and *Lawrence Welk* once a week should be enough."

Lucy's comment was "But that's impossible! I haven't even tried Channel Number Five yet."

Oddly enough, after the first day or so, hardly anyone wanted to talk about the snake.

"This is crazy!" said Wilbur. "It's like we just told everybody the worst possible news in the world, and they hardly flicked a whisker; we ought to hold a general meeting at once and discuss this problem. Maybe that mouse on *Forest Friends* was just a weakling. Maybe we should start an exercise program right away!"

I agreed, but everyone else, including Albert, was pessimistic. "What good would that do?" he said. "One of us at a time against a snake, even if it's a small snake, and we're in tip-top condition, the outcome would be the same—we'd lose!"

A few days later, when the snake arrived, Mr. Adams didn't even remember that he had ordered one.

"What's that?" he said to the delivery man.

"The snake you ordered, sir," he answered. "Just sign here."

"Oh, that," replied Mr. Adams. "Just put it on the floor." And he went back to the soap opera he was watching.

Sitting on the floor, the crate looked ordinary enough. But we all knew what was inside.

"Maybe Mr. Adams will just forget to open it," said Tony.

"Fat chance!" said Albert.

"Can you smell anything?" I asked Wilbur.

"Yeah, Supernose, what do you smell?" repeated Albert.

"It's kind of hard to tell," replied Wilbur, who, of all the mice in our cage, had the most highly developed sense of smell. "The crate has such a strong scent of pine. But wait . . . yes . . . there it is . . . something I've never encountered before. . . . It must be the snake!"

"Let me get up on your shoulders, Pearl," demanded Tony. "Maybe I'll be able to smell it from up there."

"No," I said flatly.

"Oh, please? Pretty please?" pleaded Tony, and he started climbing on top of me.

I lost my temper and gave him a shove.

"What a pest you are!" I snapped. "If I were Mr. Adams, I'd feed you to the snake first!"

It was a mean thing to do and say, and I was sorry for it right away.

Mr. Adams's chair creaked as he got up to unpack the crate. First he cleared off a space on the shelf just across from our cage and washed a large tropical-fish tank that he didn't use anymore, then he opened the crate with a crowbar.

Inside was a lot of newspaper and a huge cloth bag. The bag was tied on the top with a piece of twine. As Mr. Adams untied the knot I couldn't help but notice how knobby his fingers looked.

When the snake's head appeared, hissing and flicking its tongue, Tony cried out, "I'm not scared! I'm not scared!"

Slowly Mr. Adams pulled the snake from the bag. It was like watching a magician pull silk scarves from his sleeve; it seemed to never end. At last the snake's tail came out of the bag.

"I guess we'll just have to be brave!" said Tony in a shaky voice.

Mr. Adams unwrapped the snake, which had somehow gotten coiled around his right arm and shoulder. Then he put the snake in the aquarium with a piece of driftwood and a dish of water.

None of us could take our eyes off the snake. At first he just lay there completely still. Then he started to move, sliding over himself like a greased rope. Slowly he wound himself around the driftwood.

"Now, I bet you're hungry after that long trip," said Mr. Adams, and he turned toward our cage.

That was all we needed to hear. Suddenly there was

a stampede away from the door. At the back of the cage it was sheer chaos. Everyone was trying to get as far from the door as possible.

Wilbur and I had already discussed what we would do in such a situation. We dived under the cedar shavings, hiding ourselves from view. Then we tucked our tails under our bellies and waited. At any moment I expected Mr. Adams's bony fingers to haul me up and deliver me over to the snake. Instead, I heard a heart-wrenching cry:

"Help!"

The high-pitched helpless squeak was unmistakable. It was Tony! I climbed out of the cedar shavings just in time to see Mr. Adams pull him from the cage and drop him into the snake tank. The expression on Mr. Adams's face was one of complete indifference, as if he were dropping a piece of paper into a garbage can. He didn't even care enough to stick around and watch. He put a piece of wire mesh over the tank, placed a book on top of that, and went back to his soap opera.

As soon as Tony's feet touched the bottom of the tank, he ran to the corner farthest from the snake.

"That's it! Stay away from him!" I shouted, even though I knew he couldn't hear me.

The snake turned his head in Tony's direction. His smoky yellow eyes seemed to smolder for a moment, then he looked away.

When Albert crawled out of the cedar shavings, I ran over to him. "What happened? I thought Tony was over by you?"

"That little brat!" Albert was fuming. "I told him to run!"

"You mean, he didn't take cover?" I asked.

"I don't think so," said Albert.

"BUT WHY?" I screamed.

"I don't know," said Albert.

"Yes, you do!" I insisted.

"Well, yesterday he came over to the water bottle and was going on and on about some Supermouse cartoon he saw," said Albert. "He kept saying, 'Heroes don't run. Brave mice are never afraid.' I should have set him straight, but I was kind of busy at the time."

"Darn you, Albert!" I cursed. I was so angry, I felt like biting him.

Just then Wilbur came over.

"Oh, Pearl!" he said. "I feel so bad for little Tony. But look!" He led me over to the edge of the cage and pointed to the tank.

"No, I don't want to look," I said. "I can't bear to see it happen."

"But, Pearl!" said Wilbur. "Look at the snake! He has a big bulge in his belly. To anyone who watched *Forest Friends* that could mean just one thing—he must have eaten recently. They probably fed him just before they shipped him here. So Tony still has some time . . . a few days—maybe even a week!"

"And then what?" I moaned.

"I don't know," replied Wilbur. "But a lot can happen in a week, so let's not give up hope."

With that in mind Wilbur and I climbed up to the

top of the cage and shouted up to the canaries:

"My brother is in trouble! Can you help us?"

"What? Who?" they chirped.

Pet store canaries are not too smart. We wanted them to knock some birdseed out of their cage so it would fall into the snake's tank below. They were very obliging, but we never could make them understand that the birdseed wasn't for the snake. Some of the seeds were too large and bounced off the wire screen. Luckily, enough fell through to keep Tony alive for a week. More than that he wouldn't need.

That night, while everyone else was watching TV with Mr. Adams, Wilbur, Albert, Lucy, and I sat on the other side of the cage and watched Tony.

He looked dreadfully scared as he crouched behind the snake's water dish, keeping one eye on the snake at all times. Whenever the snake moved, Tony made sure he stayed out of his way. The snake, on the other hand, seemed to ignore Tony totally. He was more interested in exploring his new home. Again and again he thrust his long muscular body along the glass and poked at the screen above.

"Doesn't he look sinister?" said Lucy. "Kind of like Peter Lorre, Bela Lugosi, and a Boscar Monger hot dog all wrapped up in one. I wonder if he's going to molt soon?"

"I don't give a hoot about him," I said. "It's Tony I care about."

"Yeah," said Albert. "The kid must be having a hard time of it. If only we lived in a tank, I could write a message to him on the glass. We could chew up mouse pellets and mix it with water to make ink."

"What good would that do?" I snapped. "And what would you write anyway? 'Having a nice time, wish you were here'? "

Albert didn't reply, but I could see the fur on the back of his neck bristling.

After closing, Mr. Adams tied back the faded cloth curtains that separated the shop from the back room. While watching TV over his shoulder he cooked his dinner over an old kerosene stove. He eats hot dogs, canned soup, potato chips, and all kinds of junk food. He doesn't drink beer or anything like that, but you can usually smell Hostess Twinkies on his breath. When it's time to go to bed, he unfolds a canvas army cot and turns off all the store lights except for the one on the tropical-fish tank. It hums all night long and gives off an eerie green neon glow.

In that light we could hardly see Tony at all. After a while Albert and Lucy went off to work out on the exercise wheel. Wilbur and I kept watch.

Now and then a car would go by outside and shine its headlights into the pet store. A big square of light would start out at the far wall by the water pipes and then sweep down past the dog-and-cat-toy display, getting smaller as it went. When it got to the hamsters, it would shoot across the floor, shine into the rabbit hutch, skim across the counter, and disappear just before it reached the snake tank. But a little gleam of light reflected off the chrome stripping on the countertop. It wasn't much; just enough to make Tony's eyes glisten in the dark.

How I wished I could talk to my little brother. I wanted to tell him how sorry I was. I wanted to tell him everything was going to be all right.

"Listen," I said to Wilbur. "Tomorrow if a customer comes in and wants to buy a mouse, everyone's going to want to get bought."

"You'd better believe it!" said Wilbur. "And that includes you and me."

I snuggled closer and whispered in his ear. "Well, I've got an idea. . . . Everyone's going to run to the door, right?"

"Right," said Wilbur.

"Now, you might get there first, and you might not. So if you really want to get bought, you've got to have another plan."

"You got one?" asked Wilbur.

"Yeah," I said. "It goes like this . . ."

(3)

THE FIRST CUSTOMER TO COME IN THE NEXT DAY WAS a little girl in a green dress. She bought a porcelain windmill for her goldfish. Mr. Adams took a long time to ring up her sale because he was watching the last few minutes of *Love of Hospital*. The little girl didn't seem to mind much. She just browsed around the store. When she came over to our cage, we all started yelling:

"Buy me! Buy me!"

"Buy a mouse! We're such great pets!"

"As far as I'm concerned, you can have me for nothing!"

"What noisy mice you have!" she said to Mr. Adams. "Do they always squeak so much?"

"Huh?" said Mr. Adams.

As she left the store, we jeered after her.

"Dumb girl!"

"Get lost!"

At noon, when Mr. Adams fed everybody, he glanced at the snake tank and noticed that Tony was still there.

"Not hungry, eh? Well, don't worry. Your dinner will be there when you want it." When he saw the birdseed on the bottom of the snake's tank, he yelled, "Filthy canaries!"

As the day wore on and customers came and went without buying a mouse, the atmosphere of gloom in the cage began to thicken. Some just sat and stared. Others paced back and forth nervously. Bitter arguments broke out over little things like snoring or taking too long to get a drink.

Later that afternoon the snake began to move toward Tony, who was taking a nap. As soon as he nudged Tony's tail Tony jumped straight up and landed in the water dish. The snake did not seem perturbed in the least. He just kept sliding along the floor of the tank as if Tony were not there at all.

Almost as soon as Tony landed in the dish, he jumped out again. Then he ran up the piece of driftwood and shook himself. Even when he was dry, he kept shivering. From there he jumped up to the wire screening and walked upside down to the edge of the tank. For the first time it seemed as though the snake really took notice of him. Flicking his tongue, he arched his head and stared into Tony's eyes. All of a sudden Tony let go and fell to the floor of the tank, bouncing off the snake's coils and running back to his hiding place.

We spent that night the same as the night before: watching Tony.

"I wonder what he's thinking," I said.

"He's probably too scared to think," replied Albert.

"If only we could devise a scheme to save him," said Wilbur.

"Sure, Mushbrain!" snapped Albert. "All we have to do is rush Mr. Adams and tie him up with the dog leashes. Then we could free everyone in the place and hop a flight to the Caribbean!"

"You've got a lot of nerve talking to Wilbur like that!" I said. "It's your fault Tony's in that tank in the first place! If he had mentioned that hero baloney to me, I would have given him a good talking to."

"Oh, yeah?" snapped Albert. "Well, let me tell you a thing or two. First of all, if it wasn't Tony in that tank, it would have been someone else. And don't think for a minute you're kidding anyone—you're glad it's not you! And second of all, you're the one who was taking care of Tony. If you'd been doing your job right, you would have known what was going on. So don't put all the blame on me! It's your fault just as much as mine—even more!"

I was just about to defend myself, claws and teeth if need be, when Wilbur calmly stepped in between us.

"C'mon you two! Arguing like this isn't going to help anyone. What's done is done."

I felt like I had a lot to say, but when Albert backed off, I did too.

That night Wilbur and I tried to get to bed early so we could be alert in the morning when the customers came in. Wilbur fell right to sleep, but I was up past midnight. I closed my eyes and lay perfectly still. I even tried my old trick of imagining someone cutting cheese and counting the slices. But all I did was toss and turn, thinking of things I should have said to Albert.

Early the next morning a young boy strolled into the store. I remembered seeing him several times before. I guessed that he was nine or ten years old. He had curly hair and freckles, and he almost always wore a T-shirt with the number forty-four on it.

"It's number forty-four—the Browser!" said Wilbur as the boy approached our cage.

"But I don't think he's browsing now!" I said. "Look how he's holding his hand in his pocket. I'd bet my tail he's got money today!"

The boy leaned forward and looked into our cage. To mice, people's faces always look bald, so I can't really say he was good-looking. But I did like his freckles and the curly hair that poured out from under his baseball cap.

"Would anyone like to come home with me?" whispered the boy.

"Me! Me!" the cry rang out as everyone immediately started pushing toward the door.

The boy watched us for a while and then he went over to Mr. Adams.

"I want to buy a mouse," he said politely.

I WANT TO BUY A MOUSE.

Meanwhile Wilbur and I swung into action. While everyone else elbowed their way around the door, we ran to the exercise wheel.

First, we positioned ourselves under the wheel, lying on our backs so we could spin it with our feet. It was slow going at first, but then the wheel really got going.

"Faster!" cried Wilbur.

"I'm going as fast as I can!" I panted.

Now Mr. Adams and the boy were both standing in front of our cage.

"My mom doesn't want me to breed them," said the boy, "so she said I could only get one."

Wilbur and I looked at each other and our hearts sank, but we kept on spinning that wheel.

"You can have a second mouse for half price," said Mr. Adams. "In case one dies, you'll have a spare."

"Sounds like a good idea to me!" squeaked Wilbur.

The boy thought for a moment, then he shook his head. "No, I'd better just get one," he said wistfully. "But it sure would be nice to have two."

"Oh, go ahead, get two!" said Mr. Adams. "Your mother will understand."

"No, she'll get angry," said the boy firmly. "She wasn't too keen on the idea to begin with. Just one will do."

"Okay," said Mr. Adams, and he reached out to open the cage door.

By this time Wilbur and I had climbed up the side of the cage and were hanging upside down above the still spinning exercise wheel.

As the door opened and everyone else on the floor of the cage pushed forward, Wilbur shouted:

"Now!"

At the exact same moment, we let go of the cage bars, turning ourselves in midair and dropping down onto the exercise wheel feet first. As soon as we made contact with the rapidly revolving wheel, we pushed off and were flung into the air toward Mr. Adams's hand.

Plop! I landed right in his palm.

Wilbur was not so lucky. He banged into the door and fell back into the cage.

"Well, I never saw anything like that before!" remarked Mr. Adams.

The boy had already picked out a cage. He held it open as Mr. Adams placed me inside.

"Is it a male or a female?" asked the boy.

"A male," replied Mr. Adams, without really bothering to check.

"Good luck, Pearl!" cried Wilbur. "I'll miss you!"

"Anything else?" barked Mr. Adams.

"Yes!" said the boy. "A bag of cedar shavings."

"You got money to pay for all this?" inquired Mr. Adams, leaning forward and scowling.

"I sure do!" said the boy, and he proudly withdrew a ten-dollar bill from his pocket.

"Humph!" mumbled Mr. Adams, and he pushed the buttons on his cash register.

Clang! Clang! Trrricket Terrick! the cash register resounded in my ears.

The boy took his change and put it in his front pocket. Then he picked up the bag of cedar shavings and me in my new cage.

"Thanks, Mr. Adams," he said.

"Yeah, yeah. Enjoy your mouse, kid," he said as he turned up the volume on the TV.

I guess I should have been happy, but all I could think about was Tony. As we walked past the snake tank I called down to him:

"Tony, don't worry. I'll come back to get you. I promise!"

(4)

As soon as we stepped out onto the street, the boy held my cage up to his face and said:

"You know what? You're my first pet. I've never even had a goldfish before. But don't worry. I'm going to take good care of you."

Just then a girl on a skateboard zipped past.

"Hi, Jay!" She smiled.

So Jay's his name, I thought. I wonder what name he'll give me.

As we went down the street I tried to make a mental note of all the buildings we passed. I also concentrated on the exact sequence of smells we encountered. First there was a shoeshine parlor, then a delicatessen that smelled of pickles and corned beef, then came the gasoline smell of a garage mixed with the sweet aroma of the bakery next door.

Bang!

I heard a loud noise. It startled me so, I jumped straight into the air and hit my head on the top of the cage.

"Now, what came first?" I asked myself. "The delicatessen or the shoeshine parlor?"

"Take it easy, mouse!" said Jay. "It was just a car backfiring."

"Oh, shut up!" I squeaked at him. "Can't you see I'm busy remembering?"

About three blocks from the pet store we turned left and went past a construction site. Sitting on a platform above the street were some workmen eating their lunches.

"Hey, kid!" yelled one of the men. "Whatcha got there? Lemme see!"

He was a beefy-looking man with a stubby beard and a cigar in his mouth.

"It's a mouse," said Jay, turning my cage for the man to see.

"Real cute! Whatcha gonna call her?"

"It's a boy mouse," said Jay. "And I haven't thought of a name yet."

The man took a swig of coffee from his Thermos and wiped his mouth on his sleeve.

"Why don't you call him George!" said the man with a grin. "After me!"

Jay thought for a moment, then he nodded his head in approval.

"George. I like that."

The man's grin grew even wider now as he poked one of his buddies in the ribs.

"Hey, Joe!" he crowed. "Did you hear that? The kid's gonna name his mouse after me!"

"George," said the other man with a wry smile, "that's a good name . . . for a mouse!"

Jay was in a cheerful mood. As we walked away from the construction site he began to hum a tune to himself. It was a simple melody that he repeated again and again. Gradually he added some words to the song:

I got a mouse.
I got a mouse.
Gonna take that mouse
To my house.

Every time he came to a curb, he jumped instead of stepping down to the street. It wasn't a big jump, just a little hop. Every time he hopped, he sang the words:

Yes, I am.
Yes, I am.

We walked for six blocks and then turned right at a drugstore. The drugstore didn't have a strong odor like the deli, but it was a distinctive one: a mixture of medicine, newspaper, perfume, and tobacco.

We walked for some time down this new street, passing fewer stores and more houses. Then we came to a bridge that crossed over a big river. The smell of the river was delightful, and the gurgling sound it made was a pleasant change from the harsh noise of the traffic.

On the other side of the river there were no stores, very few houses, and lots of trees.

I couldn't help but marvel at the trees. I had seen trees on TV before, but it was nothing like seeing the real thing. As they arched overhead their multicolored leaves seemed to fill the entire sky.

"We're almost there, George," said Jay, interrupting his song. "I think you're going to like it here, George. I've got my own room, and you can share it with me."

I winced to hear myself called George again and again.

Finally we turned into a stone driveway, walked across a big green lawn, and entered Jay's house.

"I got the mouse!" called Jay.

"Oh, really?" said Jay's mom, who was seated at the kitchen table sorting out coupons.

Jay held me near his mom and we examined each other. She had a small round face and deep green eyes just like Jay's. For a human she looked rather nice, but obviously she didn't think much of me.

"Cute," she said. But I could tell from the sour expression on her face that she didn't like mice at all.

"Don't worry, lady!" I said. "I don't plan on being around here very long."

As Jay picked up my cage and started to leave the kitchen, she called after him.

"Now, don't forget. You promised to keep him in your room and clean the cage twice a week! I don't want that rodent getting loose or smelling up my nice clean house!"

"Don't mind her," Jay said to me in a hushed whisper. "She just gets hyper sometimes, that's all."

Jay carried me up the narrow staircase that led to his room. It was a tiny room with a sloping ceiling, one small window, and lots of posters on the walls.

"Now, where shall I keep you?" said Jay. "Ah, yes. My bureau!"

Jay's bureau was already cluttered with junk. He cleared off a space for my cage by sweeping some of it into a shoe box and storing it under his bed. Still, there was barely enough room for my cage. On one side I was shoved up against a model airplane, a box of baseball cards, and a Mason jar containing bottle caps. Along the back of my cage I had an excellent view of Jay's shell, string, sticker, and rock collections.

"I collect things," said Jay. "I also have a paper route. That's how I got the money to buy you. To tell you the truth I was thinking of getting a dog, but Mom said they cost too much to feed. I wouldn't want to have one if I couldn't feed him right."

A dog indeed! I couldn't for the life of me figure out why anyone would want a dog. From what I had been able to gather just from watching TV, they are not only expensive, but spoiled and destructive too. They get hair all over the furniture, chew and dig up everything in sight, and when they get sick, it costs a fortune at the vet's to get them well again. I think Poppa said it best: "They say a dog is man's best friend, but when have you ever seen a sign that says 'Beware of Mouse'?"

"Last year we had a pet mouse just like you in our classroom," said Jay as he opened the bag of cedar shavings. "So I know all about how to take care of you."

Jay opened his closet door and slid out an old cardboard box that was filled with boots. He dumped the boots out and kicked them back into the closet.

"This year I'm in Miss Anderson's class," he said as he placed the box on his bed. "She doesn't like to have pets in the classroom. When we asked her, she said maybe this year we'd visit the zoo instead. Billy Chase said, 'Better phone ahead and let all your relatives know you're coming!' Billy sits right next to me. His uncle was almost a major league pitcher, but he hurt his arm in a motorcycle accident. Imagine that!"

It was hard to follow everything Jay was saying, but I liked the sound of his voice. Mr. Adams sure never talked to us like that.

When Jay opened my cage door, I instinctively jumped back, but he quickly cornered me and grabbed my tail. Then he lifted me out of the cage and lowered me into the cardboard box.

My first thought was escape. I jumped as high as I could, but the walls of the box were just too high.

"Don't worry," said Jay. "I'll have you out of there in a jiffy. Just have to fix up your cage first, that's all."

I COLLECT THINGS.

While Jay was working on my cage I tried pushing my way out the bottom of the box. When that didn't work, I started chewing. I found a spot underneath one of the bottom flaps where Jay wouldn't notice my teeth marks.

By the time Jay was ready to put me into my cage, I had made considerable progress. A few more minutes and I could have chewed my way through.

Now the floor of my cage was covered with a thick layer of cedar shavings. There was a piece of carrot, some celery, and some sunflower seeds in my food dish, and my water bottle had been filled.

I inhaled deeply and smelled everything. So this is real food! I thought. No more mouse pellets for me!

First I tasted the carrot, then the celery, and finally the seeds. It was like chewing and swallowing a rainbow! When I was thoroughly stuffed, I went over to the water bottle and had a little drink. It was such an odd feeling, drinking from my own water bottle. The water tasted pretty much the same as pet-store water, but it was so nice knowing that I'd never have to wait my turn to get a drink or be rushed by someone else.

Then Jay opened the cage and placed a white cup in one corner. Next to the cup he put two tissues. I went up to the cup and rubbed it with my whiskers. It was so smooth, it tickled. The tissues had a perfume smell that I'm sure Lucy would have loved. I pulled them into the cup and began tearing them up to make myself a cozy little bed.

All the while I worked Jay watched quietly and said nothing. His face was pressed up so close to the bars, I could see myself reflected in his eyes. Although I was looking at Jay, I kept thinking about Adams's Pet Store, wondering how everyone was, and worrying about Tony.

"It must be nice to be a mouse," said Jay. "You look so cozy in there. I'll bet you haven't a care in the world."

(5)

Later that evening Jay opened my door and put his hand inside my cage. When you're as small as I am, even a kid's hand looks scary. I knew the friendlier I was with Jay, the better my chances of escape. So I ventured forth. First I just sniffed his fingers. Then I climbed aboard.

"Gee, your feet are cold!" exclaimed Jay.

For some time Jay held his hand steady and just talked to me:

"Sorry I couldn't spend more time with you this afternoon, but I promised to help Mr. Williams clean out his garage. I made two dollars and fifty cents. So tomorrow I can go to the movies with Billy Chase. . . ."

When I decided to walk up Jay's wrist, he pulled his hand from the cage. I thought of jumping and making a run for it, but I knew he'd probably catch me, and it might be a long time before he'd trust me outside the cage again.

I'M...
BEAUTIFUL!

all kinds of things on the bed. "A little playground just your size."

I walked over to the center of the bed to investigate. There was Jay's baseball glove and his model airplane, a toy fire engine and a sports car, a reel of kite string and a bag of marbles. To this Jay added a music box with a rocking horse that rocked on top as the music played, and a small cardboard box containing Jay's twig collection.

It really was like having my own playground. Every time I stepped on the airplane wing, it tilted back and forth like a teeter-totter. I climbed all over everything and even rode the rocking horse.

Finally Jay put me back in my cage, got undressed, and turned off the light.

"Tomorrow's gonna be a great day, George!" said Jay, and he leaned over and put his baseball cap on top of my cage.

I wanted to sleep that night, but I felt wide-awake so I got in the exercise wheel and started running to tire myself out. Every once in a while I glanced over at Jay sleeping in his bed. I kept thinking. Nobody heard my promise but Tony, and he might be in the snake's belly already. Even if I do manage to escape, I'll probably get lost, eaten by a cat, or run over by a truck. Maybe I should stay right here.

(6)

JAY WOKE UP AS CHEERFUL AS THE MORNING SUN THAT was pouring in through his window.

"Hi, George!" he chirped. "Want anything special for breakfast?"

Jay got dressed and reached his hand into my cage. This time I didn't hesitate at all. I just hopped on, and he put me in his pocket.

For breakfast he had a peanut butter and jelly sandwich.

"Jelly is terrible for your teeth," he said as he scooped great big gobs of it onto his bread. "Want some?"

He put a little bit of it on his finger, and I leaned out of his pocket to taste it. It was delicious, but he didn't hold his finger there long enough for me to get more than a few bites.

"I'll bet they never fed you like this in the pet shop," he mumbled through a mouthful of peanut butter and jelly.

After breakfast Jay put everything away and wiped off the kitchen table. Actually he just knocked the crumbs onto the kitchen floor.

"Mom has a fit if I don't keep the kitchen clean," he explained. "She also likes me to do chores on Saturday mornings. That's why I have to get up early and get out of the house before she wakes up."

Jay opened the back door and sat down on the steps.

"Now, what to do . . ." he mused. "Go for a walk or a bicycle ride? A walk would be safer. . . ."

"But not as much fun!" I squeaked.

Then he stood up and walked toward the shed where he kept his bicycle. Halfway to the shed he stopped and looked down at me:

"If you were to fall, you might really get hurt," he said. "So you've got to stay in my pocket."

His bicycle was all stripped down. It didn't even have fenders. As he rolled it from the shed to the driveway it made a loud noise almost as if it had a motor, but it didn't have a motor. I couldn't figure it out. Then I saw what was making the noise. Jay had taken some old playing cards and attached them to the frame of his bike with clothespins. As the wheels turned, the cards slapped against the spokes and made a rapping sound.

He hopped on and started pedaling. It was scary at first. The faster he went, the more racket the cards and spokes made. Scared stiff, I curled up into a little ball and snuggled down deep. Then I started to get used to it. Finally I worked up enough courage to peek out of Jay's pocket.

OH, MOUSE!

Oh, mouse! What a thrill it was! Everything streaked past so fast—red, green, blue. All the colors got smeared together and swished away. It took me a while before I could even begin to figure out what I was looking at. And the wind blowing in my face—it was fantastic!

We rode around for a long time, and everywhere we went, Jay described everything—the people, the houses, the trees, even the telephone poles.

"That one's got extra spikes on it," he said. "Dennis Maloney climbed it almost to the top . . . very dangerous. There's Mr. Tarp. He's almost always drunk. See the dents on his car? His wife has seventeen cats. Now we are passing Mr. and Mrs. Oglebees'. Don't they look old? Billy Chase says they're turning into powder, but they have the biggest tree in town, and they don't mind if you climb it. And look there—that's the rock 'n' roll place. The people there live in the big city. They only come out on weekends and always have wild parties."

Finally Jay pulled into someone's driveway. He got off his bike and leaned it against some bushes.

"This is Billy Chase's house," he said. "Let's see if he's up yet."

Jay knocked on the back door and waited. Then he knocked again and waited some more. When he knocked a third time, Billy's mother came to the door in her bathrobe.

"Billy hasn't had his breakfast yet." She yawned. "But you can wait outside if you want to."

While we were waiting Jay took me out of his pocket

and set me on the grass. I thought of making my escape then, but Jay was hovering over me. All I could do was go exploring.

The grass was alive with so many things to see, taste, and smell; I had a ball just following my nose.

When Billy Chase came out wiping egg yolk from his chin, Jay showed me off with pride.

"I just got him yesterday," he said. "But he's already as tame as the one we had at school."

Of course, Billy wanted to hold me, which I didn't mind at first. But he jerked his hand, and his voice was so loud, I was really glad when Jay took me back.

After that, Billy got out his bike and we rode around some more. Once we passed some girls, and Billy wanted to stop and scare them.

"Let's dangle George in front of their faces and see what happens!" he suggested.

"I don't think George would like that," said Jay. "Besides, they probably wouldn't do anything anyway."

"Yeah, I guess you're right. Girls nowadays are tough."

After lunch at Billy's house (I had half a potato chip and some alfalfa sprouts), Jay and Billy rode their bikes to the movies.

On the way there I must have fallen asleep in Jay's pocket and I didn't wake up until the movie was almost over. What I did see of it was really neat. It was called *Space Gladiators*, and it was about some strange people and robots zapping one another and riding through the dark in fancy teakettles.

After the movie Jay and Billy parked their bikes in front of Hank's Department Store. They went in, sat down at the counter, and ordered two sodas.

I was feeling sleepy, and not hungry at all, but the place smelled so interesting, I poked my head up to have a look. When I did, I couldn't believe what I saw. Just two seats down from Jay was the skinny kid with thick eyeglasses—the one who'd bought Momma and Poppa! While Jay and Billy were drinking their soda, he came over and said hello.

"Is that a mouse I saw in your pocket?"

"Yeah. I got him yesterday at Adams's Pet Store," replied Jay.

"That's where I got mine," said the skinny kid. "Now I've got seventeen mice!"

Poor Momma, I thought. She's in a crowded cage again!

"C'mon," said Billy as he loudly sucked out the last few drops of soda at the bottom of his glass with his straw. "I was supposed to go right home after the movie."

"No, wait!" I protested. "I want to hear more about Momma and Poppa."

But that was not to be. Jay got up, and soon we were on the bikes again. All the way I chided myself:

"What am I doing wasting my time with this kid? I should be on my way to the pet store by now!"

(7)

By the time we got home, I was really furious with myself. I had been outside all day, and I didn't even try to escape! And why? Because if I jumped when we were on the bicycle, I might have gotten squashed? Because I might have gotten stepped on in the movie theater? Because Jay was always too close? No! That's not why. It was because I was too busy enjoying myself. Oh, the shame of it! What would Poppa and Momma say if they knew? I didn't want to think about it. I felt like wrapping my tail around my neck and strangling myself.

For a long while I just sat in my little cup hating myself. Then I went over to the water bottle to get a drink and got an idea instead. It was so simple, I wondered why I hadn't thought of it before. All I had to do was get the cage all wet. Then, when Jay changed the cedar shavings, I could try my luck with the cardboard box again.

Instead of drinking from the water bottle the way Momma and Poppa showed us, I put my mouth up close to the nozzle and let the water dribble out. Drip, drip, drip—as the air bubbles rose up into the glass jar the floor of my cage got wetter and wetter.

By the time Jay ate dinner, finished his homework, and came upstairs, my cage was a soggy mess. Just for an added dramatic effect, I had rolled in it, so I was sopping wet too.

"I wonder what happened," said Jay as he took the empty water bottle off the cage and examined it. "Maybe I didn't put the top on tight enough. Oh, well, that's easy enough to fix."

Then he opened the cage door and did exactly what I hoped he would do. He put me in the cardboard box.

"Sorry about the bad plumbing, George. I'll have this fixed up in a jiffy."

As soon as I saw his head disappear from over the rim of the box, I dived for the flap and started chewing. I worked feverishly; chewing a little bit, spitting it out, and then chewing some more. My only fear was that I wouldn't have enough time before Jay put me back in the cage.

But luck was with me. The telephone rang and his mom called upstairs:

"It's Billy Chase."

Once Jay was out of the room, I didn't have to worry about making too much noise. I chomped down even harder, taking enormous bites and tearing them loose.

At last I broke through the bottom of the box. A few

more bites and there was just enough room to squeeze through. Using my head as a wedge, I flattened myself out and pushed forward with my feet.

Just as I poked my head out from under the box, I heard Jay's footsteps on the stairs. I ran across the blankets, plunged down the side of the bed, and dashed across the floor—*wham!*—right into Jay's foot!

Stunned, I picked myself up, staggered a few steps, and then started running again.

"George!" cried Jay. "Where do you think you're going?"

"Adams's Pet Store!" I squeaked, and dashed out the door, down the stairs, tumbling tail over nose.

At the bottom I picked myself up. Jay was close behind. I could hear his thumping footsteps. I hadn't gone three steps when *blam!*—everything went black. Jay had thrown a towel over me.

"Gotcha!" said Jay. Holding me down with one hand, he slid the other under the towel.

Slowly his fingers came nearer and nearer, and I knew there was only one thing left to do. I opened my mouth and bit him as hard as I could.

"YEOWWW!" he screamed, and jerked back his hand.

The towel flipped over and I ran.

"George!" cried Jay. "Come back!"

I headed for the closest cover I could find, which happened to be the couch. I ran the whole length of the couch and was about to scoot down the hallway toward the kitchen when I spotted a small tear in the

GOTCHA!

fabric above my head. A perfect place to hide! I leaped up through the tear into a forest of large metal springs.

Jay jumped on the couch and looked behind it. He got a flashlight and checked underneath, but he didn't see the tear. Then he went down the hallway and into the kitchen. I heard pots and pans clanking and furniture being moved.

"George! What's gotten into you? Where are you? George?" he cried again and again.

He must have checked every room in the house and the basement too. Every time he came near the couch my heart pounded.

Then Jay's mom called from her bedroom:

"Turn out the lights and go to sleep. You'll find him in the morning."

But Jay kept searching. Finally Jay's mom came out of her bedroom: "Go to bed this minute or else!" she screamed.

"But I won't be able to sleep until I find him," said Jay.

"Then just lie down!" snapped his mom.

"You're glad, aren't you? You never liked my mouse anyway!"

"I said, GO TO SLEEP!" shouted Jay's mom, gritting her teeth.

Jay stomped up the stairs and slammed his bedroom door. For a while everything got quiet. Then I heard the muffled sound of Jay crying into his pillow.

When I was absolutely sure it was safe, I climbed out of the couch and started to search through the house. There were no lights on, but the full moon was shining through the window and made it easy to find my way around. I checked along the floor for knotholes or spaces in the molding. I didn't have any luck there, but in the bathroom I found a hole in the floor where some pipes came up from the basement. I crawled down the pipes, made my way across some wooden beams, and escaped through a crack in a cellar window.

(8)

IT WAS A CHILLY NIGHT AND MY FUR WAS STILL DAMP from the dowsing I had given myself. As I set out across the lawn toward the road I began to shiver. At the edge of the lawn I paused to collect my thoughts. The one thing I remembered clearly was crossing a river. I stood up, turned my head from left to right like a radar screen, and sniffed the air.

I wish Wilbur were here, I thought. He'd be able to smell that river.

I sniffed and sniffed. Water has a very distinctive smell, but there was so much of it around. At the end of Jay's driveway there was an old tree stump. I climbed up.

Now things looked more familiar. I made a guess which way the river was and set off down the road. I hadn't gone very far when I saw a car coming. I crossed the ditch and hid in the field as the car passed. I was about to leave the field and jump back onto the road when I encountered a very unusual sight.

I saw a small apple rolling through the tall grass in the field as if it were propelled by magic. For a moment I thought it was a ghost—or a haunted apple! As it came closer and closer I got frightened and was about to run. Then I realized there was nothing magical or spooky about the apple at all. It was simply being pushed from behind.

"Hello," I said to the plump brown mouse behind the apple.

The apple stopped rolling and the brown mouse stepped out. He was an older mouse with long whiskers and a slightly tattered left ear. He looked curiously at me out of his large brown friendly eyes. The expression on his face was one of complete puzzlement.

"Well . . ." he said at last. "You look like a mouse all right, but what happened to your fur? It's all white!"

"I'm a white mouse," I said. "Haven't you ever seen one before?"

"Nope. Can't say as I have," said the brown mouse, sitting down in front of me and scratching under his chin with his front paw.

"Well, I've never seen a brown mouse," I told him. Actually I had seen a brown mouse on TV but I didn't figure that really counted. Besides, I was pretty sure this character didn't even know what a TV was!

"Pleased to meet you," said the brown mouse. "My name is Oliver."

"And my name is Geo—I'm Pearl."

"Where're you headed?"

"Toward the river and into town," I told him.

"You know," said Oliver, pawing the ground and swishing his tail back and forth, "my wife, Josephine, would sure get a kick out of meeting you. How would you like to come over to our nest for a bite to eat?"

Anxious as I was to push on with my journey, I decided to accept Oliver's offer. I wasn't hungry, but I had caught a chill and was beginning to sneeze. Perhaps if I could get out of the cold night air for a while, I could avoid getting sick.

"I'd be very pleased to meet your wife and share a meal with you," I replied.

"Good!" said Oliver. "Our nest isn't too far. And it won't take you out of your way. I know a back route to the river. I'll show you later. Just follow me."

"What about your apple?" I asked, as he seemed to be leaving it behind.

"Oh, I'll come back and get that later," he said.

Oliver led me on a winding path through the tall grass—in, around, under, and over large clumps of dirt, rocks, and sticks. As we traveled he talked on and on, not seeming to care if I was listening or not.

"Frost gonna hit hard pretty soon," he said. "All the flowers are almost gone by now anyway. Green things turning browner every day. You should see this place in the summer. Smells sweeter than honey. All those pretty summer flowers seem to start the leaves on fire in the fall, like a match starting a bonfire. By the time the fire gets going, the match is all burnt out."

It was a pretty thought. Oliver had lots of pretty thoughts. The field was his home, and he loved to talk about it. He talked about its insects and birds and flowers. He talked about its smells and tastes and seasons and sounds.

"Everything's got its summer sounds and winter sounds," he said. "In the summer the trees rustle their leaves in the breeze like thick petticoats. And in the winter the cold wind knocks their branches together like old bones."

"How do you know what a petticoat is," I asked, "living out here in the field?"

"Oh, I've been around," said Oliver. "Lived in town for a spell. Never seen a white mouse though."

"I come from a pet store," I explained. "Everyone in my family has white fur."

"Apetstore," said Oliver, pausing to think very hard. "Don't know if I've heard of such a town."

"No, not Apetstore," I said. "A pet store."

"Oh," said Oliver. "Nice place to live?"

"No!" I answered. "It's not very nice at all."

"Is that where you're coming from?"

"Not exactly," I said. "I'm coming from a house where I lived with a little boy. I was his pet mouse."

"No kidding!" exclaimed Oliver. "Now I've definitely heard of that. Supposed to be a pretty easy life. But I guess you didn't like that either?"

"Well, actually I did," I said, attempting to explain my situation. "But right now I'm on my way back to the pet store."

"But I thought you said—"

"I know I said it wasn't so nice there. But that's why I'm going back—to help the rest of my family escape."

"Oh, I see!" said Oliver, at last grasping my situation. "Well, we're here."

I looked around, and all I saw were two large rocks and an old stump.

"We are?" I asked. "Where's your nest?"

"Well, you don't think we built it on top of the ground so every stray cat could take a swipe at us do you? It's under the rocks."

Oliver stepped closer to the two large rocks and disappeared into the space between them. When he was almost all the way in and only his tail could be seen, he called to me:

"C'mon in."

I followed Oliver into the space between the rocks. It led downward into a dim passageway. This in turn led to a large central chamber. It was unlike any place I had ever been before, yet I felt instantly comfortable there.

"Josephine!" called Oliver. "Wake up! We have company."

From out of a pile of dry brush and torn newspaper, Josephine popped up her head and yawned.

"How do you do?" she said sleepily.

Oliver led me to a place in the center of the chamber.

"Sit down here and rest awhile," he said. "Josephine and I will get you some dinner."

For a while Josephine just stared at me.

AMICE
AMICE
AMICE

"Don't that beat all?" said Oliver. "Her whole family has white fur. And oh, I almost forgot. Her name is Pearl. Pearl, this is Josephine."

"I think your fur is quite becoming," said Josephine. "And I like your name too."

What a nice mouse she is, I thought, and returned the compliment.

Josephine just smiled. Then she crawled out of her well-padded bed and helped Oliver prepare a meal.

On the floor in front of me they placed three leaves: in the middle was an oak leaf with two smaller willow leaves on either side.

All around the main chamber were small alcoves that served as storage spaces for food. One space had nothing but dried corn; another had roots and wild seeds; still another contained scraps of people food—dried crusts of bread and bacon rinds. In one alcove there was even an eggshell that served as a bowl. It was filled to the brim with wild blackberries.

On the leaf in front of me they placed a sampling of all the different kinds of food they had. On their leaves they placed only dried corn.

When all the food was set out, Josephine and Oliver sat down next to their leaves and Oliver began a prayer.

"Dear Lord of mice and men," he said, bowing his head and closing his eyes. "We thank You for this food we are about to eat. I know You worked hard to make it, and I'm sure it's going to taste very good. Amice."

"Amice," said Josephine.

"Amice," I repeated after her.

It was the first time I ever heard a mouse say a dinner prayer. I guess the idea of saying a prayer over a mouse pellet had never occurred to any of us.

As we were eating, Oliver talked on and on. He recounted the entire tale of how we met and everything we said. Josephine, on the other hand, asked a lot of questions. She wanted to know all about my family, the pet store, and even Mr. Adams.

"I just don't understand why one man would want so many animals for pets," she said.

"He doesn't keep us for pets," I explained. "He sells us."

"Is he a nice man?" asked Josephine.

"Momma said he used to be. When Mrs. Adams was alive, he always kept the shop in tip-top condition. Once in a while he would even slip us a carrot to nibble on. But after Mrs. Adams died, he just gave up on life. All he cares about now is watching TV."

"That's sad," said Josephine. "Very sad."

The dinner they served me was truly delicious. The dried corn and stale bread were as good as anything Jay had ever given me. The wild seeds had a nutty flavor I especially liked, and the berries were scrumptious. I didn't think I was hungry when I sat down to eat, but I soon finished everything on my leaf.

While Oliver talked on, Josephine got up and gave me a second helping of everything. When I finished with my second helping, she asked me if I would like some more, but by then I was full. Perhaps I had eaten too much, too fast. In any case I was starting to feel ill.

"Why, you're shivering, my dear!" observed Josephine. "Come lie down in this bed and warm yourself."

She led me to a corner of the nest and had me lie down in a soft pile of milkweed. She and Oliver pushed the fluffy milkweed all around me, but I still felt cold.

"This girl has a fever!" said Oliver. "I'll go and gather some herbs right away."

Oliver turned and was almost out of the nest when Josephine called to him:

"Don't forget the coltsfoot leaves! There are still a few growing near the big rock at the edge of the brook."

By this time I was shivering so much, my teeth were chattering.

"Don't you worry," Josephine reassured me as she wiped my brow. "Oliver and I will take good care of you."

For a while I was freezing cold. Then I started to get hot. By the time Oliver got back with the herbs, I was delirious.

"Chew this," he said, holding out a leaf. "It will make you better."

I took the leaf in my mouth and chewed it. It smelled nice but tasted bitter. I chewed and swallowed as much as I could stand.

"Good," said Oliver.

"Now, get some rest," said Josephine. "Oliver and I will take turns watching over you."

I closed my eyes and soon fell into a restless, troubled sleep.

(9)

By the next morning I was feeling a lot better, but Josephine wouldn't let me get out of bed.

"You've got to rest!" she said.

I tried to stand up but my legs were too shaky.

"But I have to—ACHOO!—get going," I said.

"It would be smarter if you stayed here and rested. You might catch pneumonia if you try to leave too soon," said Josephine.

"I guess you're right," I answered, and lay back in my bed disgusted with myself for having gotten sick.

"Here, try some of this. It's a special herb I found."

I nibbled on the herb she offered me. It tasted a lot better than the one I had last night.

"Don't eat too much," said Josephine. "Sometimes a little medicine is more powerful than a lot."

Josephine's medicine was extremely powerful. First it made me very thirsty. Josephine brought me grass blade after grass blade covered with dewdrops. Then I started sweating all over and shaking. It was certainly scary, and I don't know what I would have done if Josephine hadn't been there to reassure me.

"It's just the medicine doing its work," she kept saying.

After that I fell asleep for a while, and when I awoke, I felt much better. But when I tried to get up, my muscles ached so much, it felt as if a mountain were leaning on me. I flopped back into my bed and looked up at the stone walls. "Pearl, you sure picked a lousy time to get sick," I said to myself. As I was lying there I heard Oliver in the passageway.

"You darn apple!" he cursed. "You know you can fit through here. Now, pull in your gut and roll!"

"Quiet down!" hushed Josephine. "Pearl is resting."

"Sorry," said Oliver, lowering his voice. "It's this blasted apple. I can't fit it through the passageway, and now it's stuck."

Josephine went over to the apple. She wrapped her tail around the stem and told Oliver to give a push.

"Okay!" she said. "On the count of three you push and I'll pull. One, two, three!"

I could hear Oliver on the other side, grunting and groaning as he pushed. Josephine pulled hard, too, but the apple didn't move.

"I guess we'll have to chew it in half," said Josephine.

"But if we do that, it won't last as long. Let's try it again," suggested Oliver.

This time Josephine dug her claws into the ground and yanked with all her might.

I heard the apple's shiny skin squeak against the stone walls of the passageway and then—POP!—it rolled into the main tunnel, knocking Josephine to the ground.

"Good work!" said Oliver as he strode into the nest smiling. "That should last us till December!"

The rest of that day I stayed in bed, getting up only to eat my dinner. That night I felt one hundred percent better. A little weak perhaps, but strong enough to travel.

When I told them I was leaving, Josephine said:

"You really should rest another day."

"My little brother Tony may not have another day!" I explained.

"Well, then, let us walk you part of the way to the river and point you in the right direction. It's the least we can do," said Oliver.

Before we left the nest, Josephine insisted that I eat a little more.

"You've got to build up your strength," she said. "It's not going to be an easy journey."

While I was eating, Oliver sat down next to me. He was very quiet and seemed lost in thought.

"Is there something on your mind?" I asked him.

"Yes, there is," he replied. "Tell me. Have you given much thought as to what you and your brothers will do once you're out of the pet store?"

"Well, no, I haven't," I replied.

"Josephine and I were talking about it while you were asleep," continued Oliver. "And we figured that if you were successful and did manage to free your family, you could bring them back here. The country would be a good place for Tony to grow up. There's a lot we could teach you about living out in the field, but it won't be easy. There's a lot of hard work to be done before winter sets in."

"We had to learn it all the hard way," said Josephine. "But at least we started out in the summertime."

"Someone will have to show you folks what kinds of foods are good to eat and what kinds are poisonous," said Oliver. "You'll have to learn how to dig up roots and find wild seeds, how to carry the food and store it safely in your nests."

"The first nest we built got washed out in the spring rains," said Josephine. "The children were just babies then. We had a lot of trouble moving them to higher ground."

"You've had children?" I asked.

"Oh, sure," said Josephine. "But they've all grown up and moved away."

"Well, that's a real kind offer," I said. "When I get back to the pet store, I'll tell my brothers what you said."

Finally it was time to go. As we left the passageway Oliver cautioned me:

"I heard an owl out here earlier," he said. "So be

WATCH OUT
FOR THE OWL.

on guard. There may not be time for a warning. If you see me dash off suddenly, stay close. We know the best places to hide."

Oliver led the way, I followed, and Josephine brought up the rear. First we marched beside a moss-covered stone wall, past an old broken wagon wheel half buried in the dirt. Then we crawled through a rusty bucket that had no bottom and jumped across a tiny brook.

"In the winter," said Josephine, coming up beside me, "you've got to break the ice to get a drink here. Sometimes it's too thick, and jumping won't do the trick." She pointed to a rock on top of a small rise above the brook. "That's when a rock like that comes in handy. Just give it a push, and it'll roll down and crack the ice for you."

Suddenly Oliver stood up on his hind legs. His face narrowed with concentration, and his ears twitched as if he were listening very hard.

"Danger!" he said and dived into the darkness.

I listened for a moment but didn't hear anything.

"C'mon!" whispered Josephine. "Run!"

She and Oliver were already several feet ahead of me. For the most part they ran in a straight line, but sometimes they zigzagged through the weeds. I followed them as fast as I could. When we reached a large flat rock, they dived underneath. I followed, but at the edge of the rock I stopped and turned, hoping to catch a glimpse of what it was I was running from. Suddenly the outstretched wings of a giant owl blotted out the sky above me. As I tumbled backward I felt a rush of wind and heard his claws scrape against the rock. Then Oliver pulled me in.

"Are you okay?" he asked.

"I'm okay," I answered.

"You should be more careful," said Josephine. "That was a close call."

Once or twice the owl tried unsuccessfully to reach under the rock.

"Later for you," he screeched, and flew into the air.

I started to wiggle my way out from under the rock, but Oliver pulled me back.

"Wait," he said. "The owl might be circling above."

So we waited, huddling together under the rock for five minutes or so. Then Oliver went out to check. When he gave the all clear, we followed.

"Well, this is as far as we can go," said Oliver. "You won't have any trouble finding the river from here."

"I feel kind of sad to be leaving," I said to Josephine. "After all, if things don't work out, I may never see you again."

"Just take care," said Josephine. "We'll be here waiting for you when you get back."

As a sign of farewell I brushed whiskers with both of them and set off on my way. Only once did I turn to look back at them.

"Watch out for the owl," said Oliver. "He may still be lurking about."

(10)

THE MOON WAS LIKE A GIANT FLASHLIGHT HANGING over my head. It was so bright, it cast shadows like the sun. This, I figured, was both good and bad. Good because I would be able to see better; bad because others would be able to see me.

I moved quickly through the weeds, winding my way toward the road. Except for the sounds of a few frogs croaking in the distance, there was little to be heard and no sign of the owl.

By the time I reached the road, the smell of the river was very strong. I hopped over the ditch and set off at a steady pace. Every fifty feet or so I'd stop and stand very still. I'd rest for a second or two; look, listen, and smell the air for any signs of danger.

It wasn't long before I came to the bridge. The river was making the same pleasant gurgling sound as it had that afternoon when Jay carried me home. But it looked different at night; the moon shimmering on its surface made me think of diamonds thrown across a silk scarf. It was so beautiful, I stopped to look at it for a while. As I stood there I let my thoughts drift with the river. Again and again it occurred to me how much my life had changed in so short a time. A few weeks ago I was just another mouse in Adams's Pet Store. I knew next to nothing about snakes and still less about what little boys were like. Back in the pet store I thought I had learned quite a lot from watching TV and perhaps I had, but now I knew it was nothing compared to being out in the world.

As I stood there staring at the water I felt scared. It seemed like my chances for success were so slight, the smartest thing for me to do was turn around and run back to Oliver and Josephine. Part of me really wanted to do that, but I couldn't; not now, not with Tony still in that snake tank.

So I gave myself a little pep talk. "Relax," I said. "The worst is probably already over. From here on it's easy sailing."

Before stepping onto the bridge, I checked to make sure no one else was coming in either direction. As I darted across, it occurred to me that this would be a good place to stop and get a drink. But first I had to get down the embankment to the water. The embankment was made of gravel and was overgrown with weeds. Slowly I descended, holding on to the weeds as I went. When I reached the bottom, I found the sandy shore of the river cluttered with garbage. To get to the water I had to walk over broken glass and through a rusted-out baby carriage. To my great disappointment the water was not very clean, but I was very thirsty.

As I bent down to take a drink I heard a step behind me.

"Hey, you!" said a harsh voice. I turned and saw the gleaming yellow teeth of a giant rat. His fur was all wet and matted, and his face seemed locked into a permanent snarl.

"Me?" I squeaked.

"Yeah, you," hissed the rat. "What are you doing down here?"

Speechless, I stepped back slowly. The rat edged closer—so close, I could smell his foul breath.

"I—I only came to get a drink of water," I stammered.

"This is my bridge and my river," he spit at me. "No one drinks here but me!"

"I'll leave right away," I said. "I won't ever come back."

"No, you won't either," he said. "Because I'm going to gnaw your pretty little ears off and then I'm going to tear you apart!"

"Please, please. . . ." I started talking as fast as I could, not knowing what I was going to say next. "My friends and I—we came down here to meet you."

"What friends?" he snarled.

"Why, the ones right there behind you," I said.

When he turned to look, I ran.

I ran so fast, I must have set a world's record. If I

HEY, YOU!

had wings, I'm sure I would have taken right off into the air. It was as if every part of me was racing on its own. My feet ran, my tail ran, my ears ran, my fur ran, even my eyeballs ran! I could hardly tell which part of me would get there first!

When I reached the top of the bridge, I just kept running. It felt as if any moment he would grab me. I ran and I ran, afraid to turn around, afraid to slow down. My heart was pounding in my ears and I was so out of breath, I thought I would suffocate.

I ran wildly up one street and down another. I didn't think about where I was going. I just kept seeing his face and knew I had to put as much distance between me and him as possible.

When I finally slowed down and turned around, the rat was nowhere to be seen. But I was lost.

Nothing around me seemed familiar. The houses, the stores, the trees . . . I couldn't recollect ever having seen a single one of them.

Now what? I wondered. How long would I have to meander through the town before I chanced upon Adams's Pet Store? I might be lost for days, weeks, even months.

For a while I wandered aimlessly, going down those streets that seemed to have more stores, hoping the streets would take me into the center of town, where I assumed Adams's Pet Store would be.

An hour later I was feeling very down and out. Here and there I noticed jack-o'-lanterns on doorsteps and porches. Some had big grins, others wore frowns. Lit from the inside with candles, their flickering faces seemed to glower at me as if they were saying:

"You foolish mouse. You arrogant silly mouse! What made you think you could save your little brother? You'll be lucky if you can keep yourself alive!"

I went up to one of them and looked inside. The warm air escaping from the pumpkin hit my face, and the bright yellow walls inside looked cheerful and smelled delicious. I climbed in through a toothy grimace and plopped myself down inside.

Walking carefully to avoid the puddle of hot wax lying at the base of the candle, I moved to the back of the pumpkin, where it was warmest. No sooner had I sat down than I saw a shadow move on the other side of the candle.

For a split second I thought it might be the rat. A jolt of fear shook me. Had he followed me here to corner me?

But it wasn't the rat. It was someone else: a dark, thin, handsome mouse with very long and elegant whiskers.

When he saw me, his eyes opened wide.

"I beg your pardon," he said politely. "I had no idea this pumpkin was occupied." Then he smiled and bowed graciously. "But I'm very glad it is! Allow me to introduce myself: Frederic French—actor *extraordinaire.* Pardon my candor, but I've never met anyone quite so beautiful as you. Might I ask your name?"

"My name is Pearl." I blushed.

Daintily he stepped around the hot wax and sat down in front of me, all the while looking at me as if he were admiring a piece of sculpture.

"I knew," he said.

I waited for him to finish what he was about to say but he just sat there looking at me. It made me feel uncomfortable.

"You knew what?" I asked.

"I just knew," he replied, gesturing boldly with his paws. "The moment I spied your fair countenance. I just knew you would have a perfectly marvelous name. And just listen to it—Pearrl. . . . Why it simply rolls off your tongue like a real pearl in a real oyster."

"Gee," I replied. "I never thought of it that way."

"Tell me," said Frederic, leaning forward, and looking very serious. "Have you ever considered a career in acting?"

"Not really," I said. "Well, maybe once or twice."

"You ought to think about it," he said. "You've got good bone structure, you know—marvelous bone structure—and the coloration of your fur . . . well, I don't have to tell you. . . . It's quite striking. Can you sing?"

"I don't know," I said, feeling somewhat overwhelmed.

"Never mind. I'm sure you have a lovely singing voice. We'll talk about your career after the performance."

"What performance?"

"Why, my performance of course! If you're going to take acting lessons from me, you'll want to see me act, won't you?"

"But you see," I tried to explain. "Right now I'm lost and I'm trying to find my way to Adams's Pet Store. You wouldn't happen to know where it is, would you?"

"No," said Frederic. "But I'm sure someone at the theater will be able to help you. Really I'm late. I only stopped in here to warm my vocal cords. A little chill can ruin an entire performance, you know."

Frederic seemed a bit strange, but since I was completely lost, I had no choice but to accompany him.

(11)

FREDERIC LED ME TO THE THEATER VIA THE BACK streets and alleys. We made our way through a group of garbage cans and cut across more than one vacant lot. Once I nearly fell into a sewer. Luckily Frederic grabbed me and pulled me back just in time.

"There's no telling where you might end up," he said, "if you were to fall in one of those things."

The theater was located on a run-down street. Most of the buildings, including the theater, looked deserted and had big boards nailed across their windows and doors. Near the front of the theater where a drainpipe hung out of the wall, Frederic leaped up onto a crate and squeezed under a loose board. I followed after him and trailed his scent for a few feet. Frederic was waiting for me near a hole in the molding inside the theater.

"Welcome to Mouse Moon Theatre," he said.

I looked around. The place was spacious and lavishly

decorated with intricate wallpaper, fancy woodwork, and enormous drapes. At one time it must have been a splendid place, but now everything was faded and torn, cracked and falling apart. Row upon row of seats were ripped open and covered with cobwebs, and huge chunks of plaster lay everywhere.

I began to notice that there were other mice already sitting on some of the seats. The closer we got to the stage, the more mice there were. Some seats had as many as five or six mice sitting on them. They sat on the cushions, the armrests, and sometimes on the back of the seats. Other mice came streaming down the front aisle.

"This is an odd place," I said to Frederic.

"Oh, indeed it is," said Frederic. "Let me tell you a little of its fascinating history. Of course, you know it wasn't always the Mouse Moon Theatre. John Barrymore and many other great Shakespearean actors played here. But alas, its day passed; the crowds dwindled and finally it was closed down. But not really! The mice who lived here all those years got to see each and every performance; and of course they learned all the parts by heart. When the theater closed down, they decided to carry on the tradition themselves. They don't charge much for admission. Each patron brings just a little food—whatever can be carried in the mouth. See over there? That's the ticket collector."

Frederic pointed to a spot near the stage where an older looking mouse stood by a large pile of food. There were bits of cheese, meat, crackers, nuts, and other delicacies stacked up higher than he was. To one side of him was a line of mice each with some food in his mouth. As I was watching, I saw the ticket collector turn away a mouse who tried to get into the theater with just one half of a lima bean. Later I saw the same mouse return with the other half of the bean. Only then was he admitted.

"But it's awfully dark in here," I said to Frederic. "I can hardly see the stage."

"Ah, my dear!" said Frederic. "Now you've touched on one of the most charming features of this marvelous establishment. Notice the skylight behind the stage. In a little while the brilliant yellow orb of the moon will rise higher and be shining through that window. When it does, a beautiful spotlight will appear on the stage. Then, and only then will the play begin. During the performance the spotlight will widen, and if everything is timed just right, the last drop of moonlight will fall as the play ends. It's really quite dramatic."

"What happens on cloudy nights?" I asked.

"The audience just moves in a little closer," answered Frederic with a chuckle. "And on really dark nights, we pretend it's radio. What makes any performance real is inspiration. Without that it is all sound and fury, signifying nothing. Take myself for example. Tonight when I play Romeo, I will draw my inspiration from our fateful meeting. I thank you in advance with this small token of my affection."

Then, without caring who might see, Frederic kissed me on the cheek! Just then a fat nervous mouse approached.

"Where have you been, Frederic?" he said, glancing

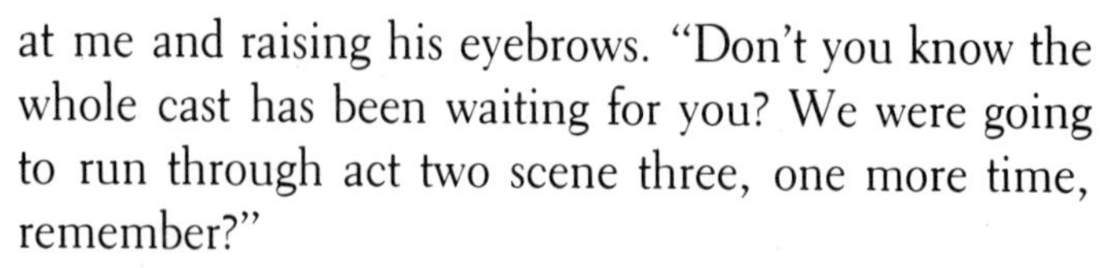

at me and raising his eyebrows. "Don't you know the whole cast has been waiting for you? We were going to run through act two scene three, one more time, remember?"

"Oh, yes." Frederic slapped himself in the face with his tail, comically. "I'd forgotten! Pearl, you must forgive me. I really must go now!"

"But what about the pet store?" I asked.

"I will make an announcement at the beginning of the performance. Mice from all over the town will be here tonight. Someone is bound to come forward."

As Frederic walked away with the other mouse I touched my cheek where he had kissed me and smiled. After looking around a little, I chose a seat in the center of the second aisle.

As I sat waiting for the production to begin, I couldn't help thinking of Frederic. I had never met anyone like him before. He was so . . . different, so cultured. No one at the pet store was anything like him. And he really seemed to like me.

In a little while, just as Frederic had predicted, the moon appeared in the skylight and a thin rectangle of light fell onto the stage.

Frederic stepped out and greeted the audience. His voice boomed out in a very unmouselike fashion.

"Tonight we present *Romeo and Juliet*, by that famous bard, William Shakespeare. Before we commence, however, I have one small announcement to make: If anyone present knows the whereabouts of Adams's Pet Store, please meet me at the end of the

ROMEO!
MY LOVE?

performance backstage. And now on with the show."

Then the play began: "Two households both alike in dignity . . ."

I loved every minute of it. It was about these two mice, one girl mouse named Juliet and one boy mouse named Romeo. Frederic played Romeo. They belonged to two different families that were always fighting with each other. In the end they took rat poison and died. It was so true to life and so sad.

After the last curtain call I jumped off my seat and headed backstage. It took me a while to push past the exiting crowd and climb the stage steps. Then I got lost among the ropes and rigging.

Finally I spotted Frederic talking with a very attractive gray mouse. As I approached I detected a familiar scent about her. She exuded a subtle aroma of pickles and corned beef.

"Ah, my Pearl," said Frederic. "Allow me to introduce Vera."

"Hi," I said.

"Glad to meet you," replied Vera. "Are you the one who's trying to find the pet store?"

"Yes, I am," I said.

"Well, you're in luck," said Vera good-naturedly. "I live just a few doors down from there in the delicatessen."

(12)

VERA LED ME OUT OF THE THEATER BY THE SAME ROUTE through which Frederic had brought me in.

"Wasn't it a beautiful play?" she said with a sigh as we stepped out onto the street. "Every time I see it, it makes me cry!"

"You've seen that one before?" I asked.

"Oh, yes, many times. And every time I see it, Frederic French gets better and better."

"I think he's a wonderful actor," I said. "And a wonderful mouse too."

"Well, I don't know what sort of a mouse he is, but I love his acting. It's so believable!"

As we scampered along side by side, Vera began telling me all about herself.

"I live alone in the deli," she said. "There are so many traps and different kinds of poison, no one else has the nerve to stay there. But the living is so easy.

There's food everywhere! It might be safer living in a church or a shoe store, but all one's time gets spent in scraping up a decent meal. And besides, there are no cats. I would never live in a place that had cats. Traps and poison are bad enough."

"What do you do with all your spare time?" I asked.

"Well, I educate myself," she replied. "Late at night I go into the library and read. I can't open the books, of course, or take them off the shelves, but oh, do I love to read the titles! Once in a while someone will leave a book open and I'll read a page or two, but it's never as interesting as just reading the title and making up your own story. I can read dozens of titles in a single night or linger over one for hours."

"That sounds very interesting," I said.

"Would you like to stop in at the library?" inquired Vera. "We'll be passing right by. I'd love to show you some of my favorites."

"No, I'm sorry," I said, apologizing. "I must get to Adams's Pet Store as soon as possible. The life of my little brother depends on it."

"Is he sick?" asked Vera.

"No," I replied. "He's been thrown into a glass tank with a snake."

"Oh!" gasped Vera. "They're deadly, and very tricky. But you're in luck again. I know someone who's an expert on snakes. Her name is Luna. She's not far out of our way, and I'm sure she'll be able to give you lots of good advice."

"But I've been delayed so many times already," I began.

"Listen," said Vera. "Snakes are more than just quick and powerful. They're hypnotists. They put a whammy on you and take over your mind. Then they just open their mouths, and you walk right in. But Luna's a psychic and knows all about that hypnotic stuff."

"Well, okay," I agreed reluctantly. "If it's on the way, it shouldn't take that much time."

"Come on," said Vera. "We can run. It wouldn't be such a bad idea anyway. This is a rough neighborhood."

Vera was a spry mouse. It was hard to keep up with her. Once I had to stop to catch my breath.

"You'll have to learn to run faster than that if you want to stay alive in town!" said Vera.

I began to notice how careful Vera was. Whenever possible she got us off the ground and led us up and over things. We traveled on fences and ledges and even rooftops. Once we had to climb down a fire escape. That was pretty scary, but Vera showed me just how to do it, and I didn't slip at all.

Finally we came to a narrow alleyway that really gave me the shivers. It was between a restaurant and a fish market and smelled terribly of cats. Even Vera seemed nervous as we tiptoed around some trash cans.

"Keep your whiskers crossed," she said. "We're almost there."

We made it through the alley, then we hopped up onto a garbage can and were about to jump onto an old fence when we saw two gray cat ears appear on the other side of the fence.

"Uh-oh! Trouble!" whispered Vera.

My first impulse was to leap down and make a run for it, but Vera held me back. At first I didn't understand why, but then I saw them—two large alley cats coming toward us.

Vera cleared her throat and swallowed. "We're trapped!" she said.

The two cats positioned themselves on either side of the trash can. I looked up over my shoulder at the fence. The gray cat was still there but hadn't spotted us yet.

"What should we do?" I asked Vera.

"Wait for them to make the first move," she replied.

Suddenly the garbage can started to rock back and forth. I looked over the rim and saw the larger of the two cats, a one-eyed calico, pushing it with her front paws.

"Come on!" she said to the other cat. "Let's give these two nice girls a little ride!"

"Yeah, boss," said the skinny black and white one with the crooked tail. "I catch your drift. . . . Have a little fun before dinner, eh?"

Vera and I hung on as they rocked it back and forth. Every time it rocked, they pushed a little harder. Any minute it seemed that the garbage can would tumble.

"Don't worry, girls," said the calico, grinning. "If you fall, we'll catch you!"

"Nuts to you!!!" sneered Vera.

"I want the white one," said the tom with the crooked tail. "I've never eaten one of those!"

NUTS TO YOU !!!

"Very bland," said the calico. "I'll take the feisty gray one."

Meanwhile the gray cat on the fence had spotted us and was getting ready to pounce.

"Don't look now," Vera called down, "but you've got some competition up here!"

When the calico saw the cat on the fence, her eyes narrowed with spite.

"Scram, buster!" she yelled. "This is our catch!"

"YEEEEOWWW!" the cat on the fence screeched, and fell from view.

In the twinkling of an eye another cat appeared in his place on the fence. This cat had long white fur and a gorgeous wide face.

"It's Luna!" said Vera. "We're saved!"

"Luna is a cat?" I gasped.

"Yeah, didn't I tell you that? She belongs to Zelda, the fortune-teller, and nobody—not even the alley cats—will mess with her."

"Okay," said Luna in a voice somewhere between a purr and a growl. "Anyone touches these mice, and the fur flies!"

"C'mon!" said the calico. "Let's get out of here!"

When they were gone, Luna's expression softened.

"This alley gives me the creeps," she said. "Follow me; we can talk at my place."

(13)

LUNA COULD SENSE THAT I WAS NERVOUS JUST BEING around her.

"Please. There is no reason to be afraid of me," she purred.

I felt so embarrassed. All my instincts told me to run, but another part of me trusted her completely.

"Don't worry," said Vera. "You'll get used to Luna soon enough."

We must have made a strange sight, we three: one large white cat followed by two mice, walking in the moonlight.

Zelda's place was indeed not very far—just one or two stores down the block.

"You see," said Vera, "we almost made it there."

"We almost made it into the stomachs of those cats!" I replied.

I had expected to see a storefront window brightly

painted with the sign of the zodiac, or perhaps a large hand within a star, but all I saw was a simple brick building with some flowerpots in the window. Above the window was a simple sign: MADAM ZELDA—READER, ADVISER.

Luna held open a small swinging trap door, cut specially for her in the front door.

Vera went in and motioned for me to follow. Only when we were both inside did Luna join us. The first thing I noticed was the smell of the place. It reminded me of flowers and perfume, but it was neither.

"What's that odor?" I asked Vera.

"Incense," she replied. "Sandalwood, I think."

Luna led us down a long hall, up some stairs, and into a small room. The walls of the room were lined with books, strange charts, and diagrams. In one corner of the room was a bed where someone was sleeping. I guessed it was Zelda. I couldn't see her face, but judging from her hair, which was long and gray, I guessed that she was rather old.

Luna tiptoed across the room and pushed past a brightly colored beaded curtain into another even smaller room. The room was empty except for a small round oak table and two stiff-backed chairs. In the middle of the table a crystal ball rested in a wooden cradle. There were no books, charts, diagrams, or anything on the walls in this room, just one small photograph of a rainbow, and a placard that read SILENCE, PLEASE.

With one graceful bound Luna leaped up onto the table, and we followed, slowly climbing up the chairs.

"You know," said Luna, pointing to the crystal ball, "it was no accident that I came to your rescue tonight. I saw what was happening right here."

As Luna spoke I looked into the crystal ball. One moment it looked perfectly clear, and all I could see was Luna's distorted face. Then I saw a flicker of light, a slight shifting of the shadows, and a filmy iridescent cloud seemed to form in the center of the ball.

"I was just waking from a little nap," said Luna, "when I felt the urge to look in here. I immediately saw you two in a storm cloud of danger. I also got the distinct impression that you were on your way to see me."

"Yes, we were," said Vera.

"It's about . . . well, perhaps you should tell her, Pearl."

"Uh . . . it's about my brother Tony," I said as I forced myself not to focus on the crystal ball. "He's been placed into a tank with a snake, and he hasn't got long to live unless I can get him out of there."

"Tell me the name of the snake," said Luna.

"I don't know his name," I replied.

"Mmmm. That makes it a bit more difficult. Can you tell me where he's located?"

"Adams's Pet Store."

"Is he the only snake there?"

"He was when I left."

"Very well then," she said, closing her eyes.

"Don't disturb her now," said Vera. "She's going into a trance."

"I'm getting a name," said Luna, speaking now as

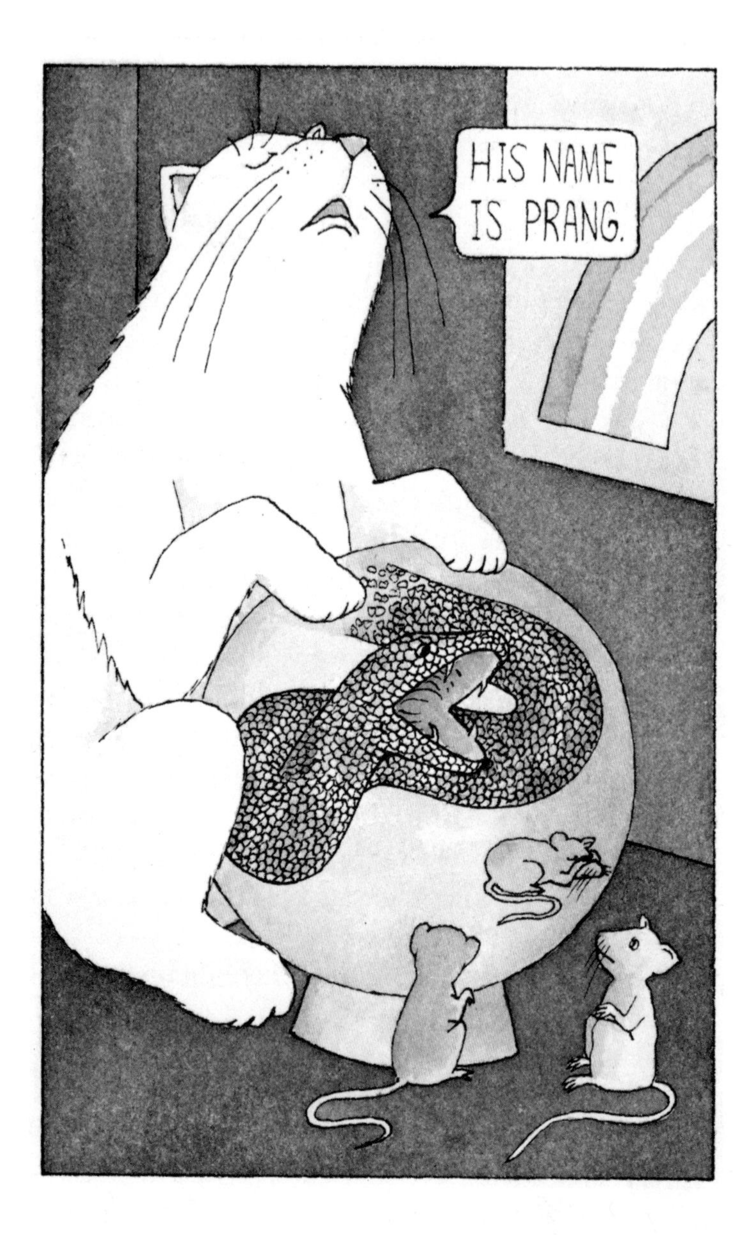
HIS NAME IS PRANG.

if from far away. "Porr . . . no . . . Paarrr . . . Prang! His name is Prang. Look into the crystal ball and tell me what you see."

I looked deep into the crystal ball; now the cloud was wavering and growing bigger. Then it started to clear up in the center, and an image formed. At first the image was fuzzy and vague. Then gradually it got clearer and sharper, and I could discern what it was.

"I can see the snake tank and my brother Tony," I said.

"Good. Very good," said Luna.

"Does that mean that my brother's still alive?"

"Does he look alive?"

"Yes, he looks kind of thin and tired, but he's still alive."

"Then he *is* alive," said Luna. "But Prang intends to eat him soon . . . in the morning when he awakens. He's quite set upon that. Nothing will change his mind, and it's a very strong mind. He was once a healthy individual, but his many years in captivity and isolation have warped his sensibilities. Now he takes delight in hurting others as he himself has been hurt."

The image of Prang grew larger and larger until all I could see was the phosphorescent glow of his eyes.

"When you encounter Prang, you must not look into those eyes. If you fail at this, withhold your name. Once he has that, he will know your innermost feelings, and there's no telling what kind of tricks he will play on you. There's not much you can do once this happens. Few victims ever survive beyond this point."

I was beginning to think that this whole visit was a big mistake. Luna's advice was interesting, but secretly I had hoped that she would give me some kind of magic charm that I could use against Prang.

Suddenly the image of Prang faded. In its place I saw two mice fighting. One black, the other white.

"It's Wilbur and Frederic!" I exclaimed. "How could they be fighting?"

"This is not a literal image," said Luna dryly, "but a symbolic one."

I guess Vera could see from my puzzled expression that I had no idea what Luna was talking about.

"Luna learned all those fancy words from Zelda," Vera explained. "She just means that what you're seeing there isn't really happening, it's more like a dream trying to tell you something."

"Yes," said Luna. "You see two mice fighting here, but the conflict is really in your heart. You're trying to decide which one will win your affections."

I hadn't really thought about it in that way before, but what Luna said made a lot of sense.

"I'm so confused," I said, "and I just don't feel strong enough to face all of this."

With her large bright eyes Luna looked at me across the table. Then she reached out and, placing her paw gently on my head, chanted:

"Like the sun that shines on a dewdrop or the tune of a songbird that fills the sky, may the clear light of love guide you through the dangerous forest of illusion to the peaceful abode of the here and now."

Just then we heard Zelda turn over in her bed.

"We should get down now," said Luna. "Zelda doesn't like me up on the table, and she might have a fit if she saw you here."

Luna jumped down from the table and we followed her through the other room, down the stairs, and into the hall.

"What about his speed and strength?" I asked.

"There is little I can help you with there," replied Luna. "Trust your own instincts. Let them lead you. There is great wisdom to be found there."

"I've been thinking," said Vera. "Maybe I should go with her."

"Most definitely not!" insisted Luna. "If my memory serves me well, your Mercury is in retrograde with Venus rising, so while this would be a good time for a romantic encounter, an escapade of this sort is highly inadvisable. Indeed, for the next few days you ought to be very careful concerning matters of personal safety."

As Luna held open the trap door and we were about to leave, I turned and said to her, "I don't want to seem ungrateful, but isn't there something else you can do to help me?"

Luna paused for a moment and then she replied cryptically:

"I merely advise; I do not lead others' lives."

On the street again Vera was supercautious. Every time we turned a corner, she had me stay back while she sniffed to see if the coast was clear.

"I'm going to take Market Street. It's a lot longer but safer," she said.

Market Street must have been the street Jay took when he brought me home from the pet store. First we passed the drugstore, then the construction site. That's where Jay gave me the name George. I remembered the man named George up on the platform eating his sandwich and drinking his coffee, and I thought of Jay at home alone in his room.

When I reached the bakery, I knew we were almost there.

"What did you think of Luna?" asked Vera.

"I guess I'll know better after tonight," I replied.

"I know she said it wasn't a good idea," said Vera thoughtfully, "but I'm willing to go with you if you want me to."

"No," I insisted. "I couldn't ask anyone to take that kind of risk. It's just not fair."

When we arrived at the deli, Vera stopped at the crack in the wall that was the entrance to her home:

"Look. I've got an idea. If everything works out, bring all your friends from the pet store here, and we'll have a celebration!"

"Will it be safe?" I asked.

"Sure it will. I'll spring all the traps first thing as I go in. Just make sure nobody eats anything unless I give the okay."

"I'd better be going now," I said.

"Be careful," cautioned Vera. "I'd hate to see anything happen to a nice mouse like you."

"Don't worry about me," I replied. "And thanks for the invite."

As I stepped out of the alley and into the street, I glanced up at the sky. The stars were still shining, but the moon was almost down. In the east the black sky was giving way to dark shades of blue.

(14)

ONCE AGAIN I WAS ON MY OWN. AFTER TRAVELING WITH Frederic and Vera, I felt confident in my ability to negotiate the street. But the town was beginning to awaken. I heard the clanking grind of a garbage truck coming down the street, and I ducked under a mailbox.

I saw a man walking his dog. Then a street cleaner swept past. It moved like a giant hunchback broom cleaning up the last few crumbs of night.

After the street cleaner turned the corner, I crept out from under the mailbox and darted down the sidewalk. In my haste I forgot to stop at the curb and check for traffic.

Halfway across the street I looked up and saw a truck bearing down on me. I froze, not knowing whether to go back to the curb or to continue. The truck—a rattling, roaring, mountain of metal—loomed up and swept over me. The wheels came so close, I could hear the hum of the tire treads echo in my ears, and I felt the street shake beneath me. But nothing touched me except the hot blast of exhaust fumes, which merely ruffled my fur.

I watched the truck turn the corner and finished crossing the street, carefully avoiding a sewer. One hop and I was on the curb, standing in front of a small brick building with large windows and a sign above the door that read, in faded green letters—ADAMS'S PET STORE.

Immediately I began searching for a way of entry. It was an old building, but there were no cracks in the foundation. To come all this way and not find a way in . . . it was unthinkable. I was about to circle around to the back of the store when I happened to glance at the front door. It was so obvious, yet I had neglected to check there. I stepped closer and examined the space between the doorjamb and the bottom of the door.

A draft of warm air hit me in the face. It was filled with all the odors of the place. I could smell everything and everyone. Each scent was more familiar than the next, and they all brought back a flood of memories. It was like seeing my whole life pass before my nose.

Pressing my chin to the doorjamb, I slid my head underneath the door. It was a tight fit, and for a moment I got stuck. I pumped my feet but that got me nowhere. So I stopped for a moment, forced myself to relax, and wiggled my way through.

Once inside I took a quick look around. From the floor everything seemed different, but nothing had changed. The green light was on in the tropical fish tanks; the bubbler was bubbling; and Mr. Adams was sound asleep, snoring loudly. But he was an early riser. Soon the sun would be up, and so would he.

I was tempted to go to my old cage first to see Wilbur and the others, but I knew I couldn't trust everyone to be quiet. Once they saw me, they'd start a commotion. Then the parakeets would squawk, the puppies would yelp, and that might wake up Mr. Adams.

I peered around the corner and saw my old cage. Some mice were up, but no one was looking at Prang. I searched for Wilbur, but he was nowhere in sight. I did see Albert though. He was over by the water bottle practicing as usual.

"Pearl! Pearl!" I heard a weak little voice call out.

It was Tony calling to me from atop the piece of driftwood. I breathed a sigh of relief. At least Luna's crystal ball was right on that score—Tony was alive. Miserable and worn-out, but alive nonetheless.

Staying clear of our cage, I jumped up onto a pile of dog food bags and leaped from one to the other. From the top bag I jumped to the counter and made my way past the turtle dish to the snake tank. As I approached all I could see was Prang's huge body pressed up against the glass.

I hopped up on a box of turtle food. From there it was just a short jump to the top of the tank.

"Don't make any noise," cried Tony in a whisper. "Don't wake him up. He said he was going to eat me for breakfast!"

HE SAID HE WAS GOING TO EAT ME FOR BREAKFAST!

I looked down at Prang. He lay perfectly still with his head tucked into his coils.

"I'm going to get this book off here," I said. "Then you can push through around the edges."

"But it's too heavy," cried Tony. "Get the others to help. Hurry!"

The book was indeed heavy, but I figured that if I could lift the cover, I could turn the pages. When I had enough pages turned, the book would pull itself over by its own weight.

It was one of Mr. Adams's old books left over from the days when he used to do things besides watch TV. Thinking of Vera, I read the title: *Gardening Made Easy* by Robert Apple Thornbee. I wedged myself under the cover and gave a shove. It moved just enough for me to slide my paws underneath. Then I pushed myself under the cover and heaved with my back. The cover flung open and hung out over the side of the tank. The hard part was over now. All I had to do was keep turning pages. I started out with the Table of Contents and worked myself through pruning, fertilizers, and grafting. As I was flipping the pages with my front paws as fast as I could, Tony called up to me:

"Can't you go any faster? I think he's starting to wake up!"

I looked down. I couldn't tell for certain, but it seemed as if Prang were edging forward.

"It won't be long now. Get ready to jump as soon as this book falls."

"I'm ready," cried Tony.

When I got to Chapter Thirteen, "Increasing Yield," the book started to teeter. I turned a few more pages and hopped off. Now the pages hanging over the edge weighed enough to pull the book over the side of the tank. Down it fell, bumping against the countertop and landing on the floor with a slap.

The puppies started yapping, the parakeets screeched, the guinea pigs squealed, and Mr. Adams rolled over in his cot.

Even before the book hit the floor, Tony leaped up onto the screening and began pushing himself underneath.

"Ssstop!" I heard a strange voice call. I looked down. It was Prang, and he was moving toward Tony.

"Don't you remember what we said to each other? It was all going to be ssso painlesss. Isn't that what everyone wantsss?"

"Prang!" I called loudly. He turned and looked up at me. His eyes seemed to whirl.

"How do you know my name?" he hissed.

I suddenly felt weak and comfortable at the same time, as if I had been dropped into a bath of warm water.

Prang glanced back at Tony, and I averted my eyes. I had distracted Prang just enough to give Tony a chance to squeeze under the screening.

"Run to the cage and let everyone out!" I called to him.

While Tony dropped down to the countertop and headed toward our cage, Prang slid up the glass and pushed out against the screen. He moved so fast, I hardly had a chance to jump down. He went straight toward Tony, so I called out his name again:

"Over here, Prang!" I shouted.

He stopped and turned slowly toward me.

"Yesss," he said with a sinister hiss.

I tried not to look into his eyes, but it was impossible, like dancing on quicksand.

"Tell me your name," he demanded. As he spoke, a crippling pain surged through my stomach.

"Tell me, and the pain will go away."

I thought of making up a name, any name, just to tell him something, but I sensed that he would know the difference. Out of the corner of my eye I could see Tony struggling with the latch. I needed to distract Prang a little longer.

"I'll ask you one last time," said Prang. "Tell me your name."

The pain in my belly was unbearable. I recognized it as the pain of Prang's own hunger which he had somehow transferred to me.

"George!" I squeaked. "My name is George."

The pain lessened but not completely.

"But you're a girl," said Prang.

"No, I'm not a Pearl!" I blurted out. The pain disappeared.

"You see?" he smiled. "I always keep my promisesss. Now, I'm coming clossser. Don't run away. I'm bringing you a present, Pearl . . . a death that is painlesss."

As soon as he spoke my name, everything around

me seemed to fade. The puppies were still barking, but they seemed so far away and insignificant. Nothing seemed real, not even myself . . . just Prang . . . and he was changing. His form faded in my mind, and his head became a hand. At first it was a gnarled fist like Mr. Adams's. Then it began to open, and it looked like Jay's hand. It was Jay's hand, and it was coming closer. As it opened up I saw Momma and Poppa inside. They beckoned to me.

"Come, Pearl," they said. "Come to us."

A wonderful light feeling overtook me, and I felt as if I were floating on a cloud—a soft, fluffy, comfortable cloud. I must be in Mouse Heaven, I thought. Only one thing seemed out of place. Momma kept sticking her tongue out at me. At first it didn't bother me much, and I didn't want to embarrass her by mentioning it. It just made me feel uneasy. Then I noticed that it looked longer and thinner than it should, and the tip of Momma's tongue was pointed in two directions. Why, it wasn't a mouse's tongue at all. . . . It was . . . PRANG!

The illusion of Jay's hand and Momma and Poppa vanished. I saw now before me the reality of Prang's grinning face; his tongue flicking in and out of a small groove under his lip; his coils flexed, ready to spring. An instant before he lunged forward, I jumped to one side. When his mouth clamped down, all he caught was the tip of my tail. I jerked it free and dashed around the snake tank.

(15)

PRANG PULLED HIMSELF UP AND GLARED AT ME THROUGH the glass. Whatever hypnotic power he had over me was gone. All I saw were two spiteful eyes and felt nothing inside.

Looking past him, I saw Tony struggling with the latch on our cage. I knew I could make a run for it and be safe, but then Prang would get Tony, so I held my ground as much as I dared, edging backward step-by-step as Prang slithered toward me. He moved slowly at first, lazily looping his coils. Then, just as he turned the corner I bumped into the turtle bowl, and he shot forward. All of a sudden his gaping jaws came straight at me and I had nowhere to go but up and over the rim of the bowl.

Klunk! Prang's head struck the side of the dish and set a wave of water in motion that knocked one of the larger turtles off his ledge and onto his back.

"Well, I've never in all my years seen anything like this!" he sputtered as he twisted his neck around to right himself. He was about to say something else to me, but as soon as he saw Prang coming over the rim of his little plastic home, he quickly pulled his head inside his shell.

I waded past him across a shallow moat onto a tiny island in the center of the bowl. There I hid myself behind two green plastic palm trees.

I waited there while Prang poured himself into the dish. Out of the corner of my eye I could see Mr. Adams sitting on the side of his cot, putting on his slippers.

When Prang was almost completely in the dish, I jumped out and headed for our cage. I didn't look to see if Prang was following me—I just ran.

When I got there, Tony was in tears.

"I can't do it! I just can't do it!" he sobbed.

Everyone was pressed against the bars.

"Hurry!" called Albert. "The snake's coming!"

I wrapped my tail around the latch as I had seen Josephine wrap her tail around the stem of the apple. Then I grabbed on to the bars of the cage with my paws and pulled, but the latch would not budge.

"Help me, Tony!" I cried. "I can't do it alone!"

"But I can't, I can't!" sobbed Tony. "And the snake is coming!"

"If you want to be a hero, now's the time to hold your ground!" I said. "Just wrap your tail around mine and pull!"

Trembling, Tony did as I asked, and together we pulled the latch free.

Wap! The door flung open and my tail got pinched. As everyone poured out of the cage like water through a sieve, I screamed in pain.

"OOOUch!"

Much to my surprise not everyone wanted to leave. "Close the door," they screamed. "The snake's out there!"

Albert freed my tail and the door snapped shut. I groaned with pain and looked up. There was Prang staring down at us. I looked for Wilbur but didn't see him. Some mice had already made their way down to the floor and were heading toward the front door. The rest of us were pinned up against our own cage cowering before the mighty Prang. His head bobbed back and forth as if he were trying to decide which one of us to eat. Soon he would strike and one of us would become his breakfast.

There were so many of us—so many little sharp teeth—I knew it didn't have to be that way. I stepped forward.

"Prang!" I bellowed. "Touch one of us and we'll tear you to pieces!"

"We will?" I heard Albert mutter behind me, and hoped that Prang had not heard as well.

"Now, move back and let us pass," I demanded, "or we'll trample you!"

"You're bluffing!" said Prang. "I've watched mice all of my life. You're nothing but a bunch of fuzzy-

TOUCH ONE OF US
AND WE'LL TEAR
YOU TO PIECES!
WE WILL?

brained twerps constantly bickering among yourselves over the smallest of trifles!"

"Oh, yeah! Well just try something and see what happens."

"Now I've made up my mind," said Prang with a smile and a flick of his tongue. "You're not as plump as some of the others, but I think you'll taste very good. The others can go free."

I gulped and looked behind me. All I saw were row upon row of blank, empty faces. Then Albert spoke up:

"Harm one hair of my sister, and you'll have all of us to deal with."

A murmur of assent rippled through the crowd. Prang's eyes widened and his head jerked back in surprise.

"Sssso, I'm to take you all on!" snickered Prang. "Nothing could pleassse me more!"

Just as I braced myself for Prang's next move, I saw a small figure dart past the turtle dish toward our cage. What a sight! It was Vera—with a gold hatpin in her mouth! She was zooming across the countertop straight for Prang! Only his lightning-quick reflexes saved him from serious injury. As he recoiled from her deadly thrust, the tip of the pin glanced off his thick scaly skin, and Vera was thrown off the countertop onto the floor.

Vera's crazed assassinlike attack had failed, but she gave us the time we needed to scatter.

Meanwhile Mr. Adams stumbled toward us:

"What's going on here?" he blared, and grabbing a broom, he began swinging it wildly at anything that moved.

"Lousy rodents!" he cursed. "I'll flush you all down the toilet!"

Tony ran by my side. Albert and Lucy followed. Together we leaped off the countertop and scrambled down the dog food bags to the floor, where Vera was waiting for us.

"You okay?" I asked.

"Sure," she said, grinning. "I've fallen from twice that height—not bad for someone whose Mercury is in retrograde, eh?"

Just then we heard a loud noise. *BOOM!*

In his frenzy Mr. Adams had knocked over his own TV set. When it fell to the floor, the picture tube exploded!

It didn't take us long to get to the door. Albert and Tony squeezed under easily, but Vera and I had to give Lucy a push. As I myself was about to squeeze under I noticed Mr. Adams hunched over his dead TV set. I couldn't say for sure, but it looked as if he were crying.

Outside I found Tony in hysterics.

"Come on, come on!" He was jumping up and down. "Let's go, let's get out of here!"

Albert was doing his best to calm him down. "Relax," he said. "The snake can't get us out here."

"Where's Wilbur?" I demanded. "I refuse to leave without him."

"You'll have to," said Albert flatly. "He got sold yesterday."

At that moment we heard a hissing sound above our heads.

We looked up. It was Prang, wiggling his way out of the mail slot.

"Run," cried Tony. "Run!"

(16)

Vera led the way down the sidewalk toward the delicatessen. When we got to the curb, she stopped to check for traffic.

"Look!" cried Albert. "He's going the other way!"

We all turned and saw Prang chasing two other mice down the street. As we watched, a car went by and nearly clipped him, but he made it safely to the other side and disappeared around the corner.

"I hope we never see him again," said Albert. "He's a mean, nasty fellow."

As we scurried down the street Tony kept saying:

"Gee, it's big out here!"

And Lucy asked of every store we passed:

"Do you think they sell perfume in there?"

When I asked Albert about Wilbur, nothing he said made me feel any better. Apparently no one had noticed how I managed to get bought. Two days later, when a pretty lady came into the store to buy a mouse, Wilbur used the same technique with the exercise wheel. This time he made it past the door.

When we got to the deli, Vera stopped at the crack in the wall.

"Now, I've sprung all the traps," she said, "but there's still lots of poison around, so don't eat anything without checking with me first. Okay?"

She made us all agree with at least a nod, then she led us inside. It was very dark, and we couldn't see much, but the aroma of good food—it was out of this world!

First Vera led us along the wall through a large machine that she said was a freezer.

"If all of a sudden this place starts shaking and making a lot of noise," she warned, "don't panic. It's just the motor. It turns on and off by itself and makes quite a racket. Don't worry though. It's absolutely harmless."

Then she led us under some tables and chairs and around a big wooden box that she called a salad bar.

"Is that like a candy bar?" asked Tony.

"Kind of," answered Vera, "but not really."

Here and there she pointed out the traps that she had sprung.

"I've seen mice get caught in traps on Saturday morning cartoons," said Tony, "and it doesn't seem to hurt them very much."

"I'm afraid real traps are quite different," explained Vera. "Until you know how to spring them, stay away, no matter how hungry you are."

"I think I'd like to learn how to spring them," said Albert.

"I'd be glad to show you," said Vera. "It's something every town mouse should learn."

"What's this delicious-smelling stuff? Can I have some?" asked Lucy, pointing to a small cardboard box containing some gray powder.

"That's rat poison," said Vera. "One mouthful will make you so thirsty you'll drink until your stomach bursts! Have as much as you like!"

"No, thanks," replied Lucy.

Vera's nest was located in the kitchen, at the back of a cupboard that was hardly ever used.

"This is where I sleep," she said, pointing to a frying pan. "It's very comfortable."

"You must be very happy here," said Albert.

"Oh, I am," replied Vera, "but sometimes it gets kind of lonely. I'd love to have some friends to share it with, but everyone I know is afraid of traps and poison."

"I could help out there," said Albert. "I know how to write. If I could just get some ink and paper, I could make little signs and put them by all the traps and poison."

Vera's eyes lit up. "You know how to write?" She gasped.

"Yes. I taught myself from watching TV," said Albert nonchalantly, even though he was very proud of the fact. "It takes a lot of practice and good tail control, but I think anyone can learn if they really want to."

THIS IS
WHERE I
SLEEP.

"I'd love to try. You must tell me all about it. But first I promised Pearl a celebration—and what's a celebration without a feast?"

"Oh, good!" cried Tony. "I'm starved! Birdseed is for the birds. I want some real food!"

On the top shelf of the pantry Vera had seven different kinds of cheese set out for us as well as coleslaw, potato salad, and pickles. Everything tasted wonderful except the pickles. Only Vera ate them.

"They're an acquired taste," she said. "Like hot mustard."

"What flavor," sighed Lucy.

"I can't decide which cheese I like best, the Camembert or the Roquefort," said Albert.

"That's easy," sputtered Tony, his cheeks puffed out with food. "They're all best!"

When some of the feasting had died down, I said to Vera:

"Tell me, what made you come to the pet store in spite of what Luna said?"

"Well," mused Vera, carefully choosing her words, "I don't like to think of myself as one who takes foolhardy chances, but even Luna says the stars impel, they do not compel. And then there was that gold hatpin. I found it one day on the floor, where some customer must have dropped it. I don't usually save things like that, but for some reason that hatpin was special. I had a hunch that someday it would come in handy, and when I thought of you fighting a snake, I knew that someday had come."

"How does it feel to be a real heroine?" asked Tony.

Vera blushed. "It feels great. Just like any time you help a friend. But gosh, I didn't do that much. Pearl's the real heroine."

I felt all eyes on me, but I couldn't look anyone in the face. "How's it feel to be a heroine?" I sighed, biting my lip. "Well, to tell you the truth, right now it feels kind of lonely."

Soon the deli opened, and we had to stay hidden all day long. Tony curled up on a small saucepan and instantly fell asleep, snoring loudly. Albert and Vera stayed up for a while talking, but then they, too, went to sleep.

I found myself a cozy coffeepot lid, and slept most of the day. But once someone opened the cupboard, and the noisy hustle and bustle of the kitchen woke me up. For a moment harsh daylight came pouring into the cupboard, bounding from stainless steel pot to copper-bottom pan, and chased away my dreams. Then someone reached in, grabbed something from the top shelf, and the cupboard was quiet and dark once again.

Soon everyone else was snoring. Everyone, that is, but Lucy and me. She came over to my coffeepot lid, and we talked for a while, mostly of Wilbur.

"Yes, I miss him," she said. "But probably not as much as you do."

"Did he say anything about me after I left?" I asked.

"No, but I could tell that he was feeling sad," said Lucy. "He just wanted to be alone. A couple of times

I caught him talking to himself. That is, I mean . . . uh . . . talking to you."

When Lucy returned to her omelet pan to get some more rest, I didn't try to fall asleep. I just closed my eyes and pictured Wilbur in my mind.

"I guess you've been talking to me now for some time, but I've been too busy to listen. So listen up now, because I've got some things to say to you. First of all, I want to thank you. You've been a true friend to me from the very beginning, and if you were here now, I'd never let you go. Oh, darn, Wilbur. Why did you have to let yourself get bought? We could have had a great life together. But I guess what's done is done. Maybe mice do have long tails and short memories, but I'll never forget you!"

That evening Vera suggested we attend the Mouse Moon Theatre. Albert and Tony were ecstatic, and so was Lucy when she found out she might be able to get some perfume there.

Vera gave each one of us a piece of cheese to use for admission. By the time we arrived, half of Tony's cheese had mysteriously disappeared, but they let him in anyway.

As we filed down the aisle we created quite a stir. Not many town mice had ever seen so many white mice before.

Lucy wanted to go backstage and ask about perfume right away, but as we were rather late, there was hardly time to find seats before the performance began.

The play was *Hamlet*. I especially liked how the

players made their tails stiff and used them as swords. Frederic played Hamlet of course, and he was just fantastic. Albert seemed to enjoy the play a lot, but Lucy kept asking when the commercials were going to come on. Tony fell asleep. After the last scene we went backstage.

"Do you really think they have perfume?" asked Lucy.

"I'm certain many of the actresses use it," said Vera. "If they won't let you have some of their own, I'm sure they'll tell you the best place to get it."

In our excitement to get backstage we somehow lost Tony.

"I'll bet he went over to where the ticket collector has his food pile," said Albert.

"Okay," I said. "I'll go get him and meet you all back there in a moment."

Sure enough, I found Tony by the ticket collector, staring at all the food.

"There's a lot of stuff in there I've never even smelled before," he said.

As I tried to pull him away an elderly mouse nudged me on the shoulder. "Excuse me," he said. "I believe I've seen several of your friends around. Did you all just arrive in town?"

Hurriedly I explained to the gentlemouse why there were so many white mice around. When I got to the part about Prang, his mouth dropped open.

"I'd heard rumors of a snake in town," he said, "but

up until now I was skeptical. I think we had all best be very careful. He sounds very dangerous."

By this time Tony had disappeared again. After an extensive search I found him in the back of the theater playing with some other young mice. They were hopping from seat to seat, giggling whenever they fell down. It was good to see Tony laughing and playing again as a young mouse should.

Finally I dragged him away from his newfound playmates, and we went backstage. At the top of the stairs we met Albert and Vera. Albert had found a dusty wall—a perfect place to demonstrate his writing skills. He had already written his name and was writing Vera's next to it.

"Where's Lucy?" I asked.

"Frederic's helping her find some perfume," said Albert, pointing past a bank of rusted footlights to a room with a star on its half-opened door.

Climbing over some ropes, Tony and I made our way toward the door. As we approached we heard Lucy's carefree laughter.

At the doorway I stopped and motioned to Tony to be silent. Frederic was dipping his tail into a bottle of perfume and applying it behind Lucy's ears. Neither of them knew that we were watching.

"Just a drop, my dear," said Frederic. "Some say too much is enough—but I say, in some matters at least, enough is too much."

"Oh, you're so clever," said Lucy.

"Yes, but one doesn't have to be clever to know beauty when one sees it," replied Frederic. "And you, my dear, are beautiful! Your bone structure, your whiskers, your ears, and now your scent—everything about you is gorgeous!"

He leaned over and kissed her cheek. Then he continued:

"Tell me, have you ever considered a career in acting?"

"Come on," I said, motioning to Tony. "Let's go."

(17)

When Lucy came out of Frederic's dressing room and announced her intentions to stay at Mouse Moon Theatre to study acting, none of us was surprised. It was as plain as the fur on her face: She had fallen tail over paws in love with Frederic. And as far as I was concerned, she could have him. Perhaps Frederic was a great actor, but he was also about as faithful as a flea jumping from dog to dog. I congratulated her and wished her well in her glamorous new career.

Then Albert spoke up. "I have some news too," he said. "I've decided to take Vera up on her generous offer to live in the delicatessen." As he spoke he gazed lovingly at Vera.

"Hurray!" cried Tony. "We're all going to live in the deli!"

"Ahem!" I cleared my throat. "That's not exactly what I had in mind. The deli could be a very dangerous place for an impulsive youngster. You might never grow up if you went to live there."

"Oh, come on!" protested Tony. "I'm not that dumb."

"It's a tricky place to live," agreed Vera.

"And besides," I said, "I know a very fine couple who live in a field just outside of town. They're wonderful mice—good simple folk—and they've offered to help us get settled. That's where Momma and Poppa would want you to grow up. I'm sure of it."

"I think Pearl's right," said Albert.

But Tony just sulked. "First Momma and Poppa, and now you—the whole family's splitting up!"

"It's just the way things happen sometimes," I said. "There's no sense in fighting it."

Tony pouted some more, putting on a sour expression as if he had just eaten a whole lemon.

"Besides," argued Albert, "I'll come and visit you in the country."

"How will you know where we live?" Tony whined.

"Pearl can give me directions, and I'll draw a map. Right, Pearl?" said Albert.

"Yes, I think I can do that," I replied. "But what about paper and ink?"

"They keep some right here," said Vera. "I saw them using it one time to make a scroll for *The Merchant of Venice.*"

As Vera was speaking Frederic came out of his dressing room and Lucy rushed to his side. I don't think he expected to see me there. He looked surprised and somewhat embarrassed for a moment, but—great actor that he was—he quickly regained his composure. He politely greeted me and then turned to Albert.

"Did I hear you discussing pen and ink?"

"Yes," replied Albert. "I understand you have some here."

"Indeed, we do," said Frederic, exchanging romantic winks with Lucy. "You're welcome to use as much of it as you like."

One thing I had to say for Frederic. He was generous.

With his help we procured the ink and paper and Albert set to work. Helping Albert draw the map refreshed my memory, and my memory certainly needed refreshing. Once or twice I had to stop and think, but with Vera's knowledge of the streets in town, the map was soon done.

As we folded the completed map and got ready to leave, Lucy seemed nervous. She kept scratching behind her ears and flicking her tail about. I guessed that she was unsure about setting off on her own and doubtful of her real acting abilities. I really had to admire her courage.

Gracious as ever, Frederic treated us to a few stanzas of Shakespeare and invited us to come back often. And when Lucy wasn't looking, he whispered in my ear: "Parting is such sweet sorrow!"

I just gave him a puzzled look and made no reply.

Outside the theater, as Tony and I said our goodbyes to Albert and Vera, a light drizzle began to fall.

?
PE
STORE
INK

Once again I thanked Vera. "When you see Luna again," I said, "tell her I said hello."

"I will," replied Vera. "And remember, you're always welcome at the deli."

"But you will come and visit us in the country, won't you?" pleaded Tony.

"Sure, we will," said Albert. "I have to test out my new map, don't I?"

Then Albert and I exchanged looks. We didn't say anything, but somehow we both knew inside that all the hard feelings and bitterness we had had toward each other were gone. We were going our separate ways, but we were still brother and sister; still friends.

(18)

THE DRIZZLE DIDN'T LAST FOR LONG, BUT SOON A HEAVY fog rolled in. I could hardly see beyond my whiskers, but that didn't slow us down very much. Most of the really important landmarks I remembered were smells anyway.

Tony was a bit slower than I, so every now and then we had to stop and rest. After passing the drugstore, I wasn't sure which way to turn, so I told Tony to sit down for a moment while I took a sniff and got my bearings.

I inhaled deeply and caught a hint of the river. Then I exhaled and inhaled again, turning my head at the same time and concentrating on direction. Just as I was pretty sure that I knew which way to go, a familiar smell met my nostrils and sent a shiver down my spine to the tip of my tail.

"Come on," I said to Tony. "Let's run!"

"Ugh! I'm tired. Let's rest a little longer," complained Tony.

I didn't want to scare him, but there were no two ways about it. I had to tell him the truth. "Prang's nearby," I said.

In a flash he was up and running. I had no idea where Prang was or if he had caught our scent, so we stayed on course and headed for the river.

As we jumped down from the curb I was tempted to stay in the road, where I knew we could make better time. But I didn't want to risk getting run over by a car, so we climbed up onto the sidewalk again.

Then with every step I noticed Prang's scent getting stronger and stronger. I felt my courage melting. Somehow I just knew he was out there in the fog, stalking us.

Halfway down the block as we passed beneath an untrimmed hedge that hung out over the sidewalk, Tony looked up and froze in his tracks. His mouth was open wide in terror, but nothing came out. I looked up and saw Prang. Draped along the bottom branches, he glared down at us with a look of deadly satisfaction and flicked his tongue.

"Ssso, we meet again!" he hissed, and dropped down on top of us. Prang could have gotten either one of us easily, but he made the mistake of trying to grab both of us at once. Like a hangman's noose his coils tightened, but we managed to wiggle free.

I knew we couldn't outrun Prang for long. He was too strong and quick for that. Our only hope was to find a hiding place too small for him to come after us.

"Over here," cried Tony.

I turned in the direction of Tony's call and saw a dim orange glow through the fog. It was a jack-o'-lantern sitting in the middle of someone's front lawn. A perfect place to hide, and Tony was already inside. With Prang just inches behind, I made a dash for it and hurled myself into the mouth of the grinning pumpkin.

Tony was hiding behind the candle. "Is—is it r-really safe in here?" he stammered.

"I don't know," I said. "The nose seems kind of large, but not large enough for Prang."

"What about the lid?" asked Tony, looking up at our bright orange ceiling.

I climbed up to take a look. Luckily it was jammed on tight.

"We're safe enough for now," I said with a sigh.

"Well, there's certainly plenty here to eat!" said Tony, picking up a pumpkin seed. "If we had to, we could stay here for days."

"Oh, yesss?" came Prang's voice from outside. "We shall sssoon sssee about that!"

First Prang tried to force his way into the triangular nose of the pumpkin, but as I had hoped, it proved too small for him to pass.

For a moment he seemed furious, then his expression changed.

"Tony, my old pal Tony," he called, softening his voice and giving it a mellow almost singsong lilt. "We

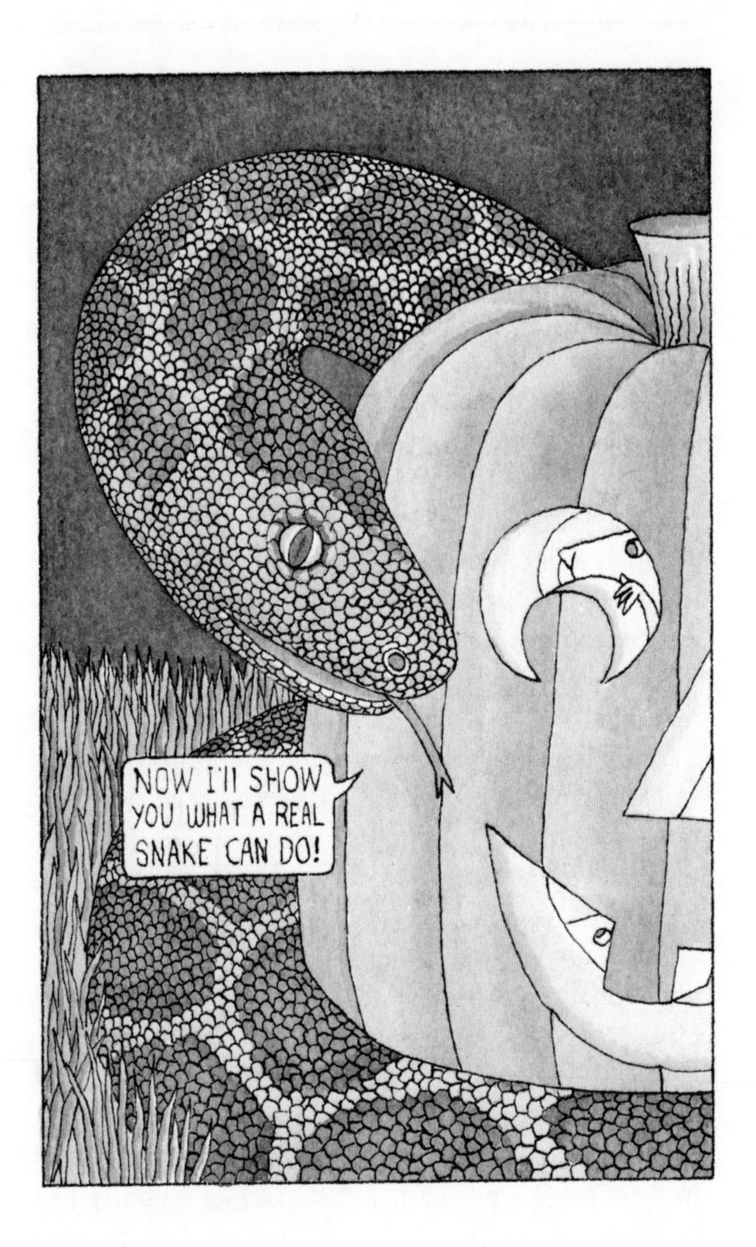
NOW I'll SHOW YOU WHAT A REAL SNAKE CAN DO!

ssspent ssso much time together. Come clossser, let me get a good look at you. It's your sssister I'm really after, you know. I wouldn't hurt you."

"No, stay back. Don't even look at him," I said.

"Don't worry," said Tony. "I know his tricks."

"Come on, Prang!" I shouted out to him. "You know you can't get us in here, why don't you just admit defeat and slink away like a nice little snaky!"

"Okay for you, sssister!" said Prang, his voice cold and mean again. "Now I'll show you what a real snake can do."

Prang's head disappeared for a moment and the pumpkin tilted forward.

"What's happening?" whispered Tony.

I edged forward and peeked out the grin. Suddenly my view was blocked by one of Prang's coils. Then the nose opening and the eyes got covered too.

"He's wrapping himself around the pumpkin!" My voice was trembling with the dire realization of what was happening.

"Look at the walls!" cried Tony. "They're starting to move!"

Suddenly we heard a terrible crack, and from every direction the pumpkin and Prang came tumbling in on us.

I really thought that was the end, but somehow I managed to struggle free. I squeezed through a section of collapsing pumpkin and scrambled over Prang's midsection. In my haste I lost track of Tony. I had gone several yards across the lawn before I heard him cry out:

"HHHHELP!"

I turned and saw him struggling to free himself from Prang's ever-tightening coils. It looked as if Tony was a goner for sure. I ran to him.

"Quick!" cried Tony, already gasping for breath. "Grab hold and pull me out of here!"

Just then a large chunk of pumpkin fell onto Prang's head. While he struggled to free himself I climbed up to Tony. Immediately he grabbed on to my shoulder and I started pulling him with both my paws and teeth. Slowly, greased with pumpkin pulp, Tony's body began to slide free.

Meanwhile Prang shook loose the chunk of pumpkin that had fallen on his head and once again began to tighten his grasp.

"I should have done this days ago!" said Prang, turning to me with a grin. "And you're next, sssweetie!"

I felt the strength in Tony's grasp growing weaker by the minute. Unable to talk, he had to struggle for every breath, while Prang kept squeezing like a vise.

I knew then that it was hopeless to try to pull Tony free. I let go and jumped down to the grass. As I choked back the tears and prepared to say my last good-bye to Tony, I noticed the candle.

Not only was it still standing more or less upright, but it was still burning! In an instant I knew what I had to do. I set my shoulder to its warm shaft and, digging my feet into the solid earth, pushed with all my might.

With surprising ease the candle tilted forward. Once or twice it sputtered as several drops of hot wax dripped onto Prang.

"SSSAAA!" he screamed, pulling away in pain. It was as if I had connected him to an electric socket. Immediately he let go of Tony and with one whiplike motion swung his head around toward me.

"Now you die!" he cursed.

But I was ready for him. As soon as he came close enough, I shoved the burning flame into his face, searing his precious tongue.

As Prang writhed on the grass in horrible pain, I ran to Tony's side.

I looked at Tony's limp body lying on the grass and a terrible thought came to me: My little brother was dead!

(19)

But Tony wasn't dead, just unconscious. I nudged him with my nose and turned him over onto his back. Slowly he began to come around.

"TONY, GET UP!" I screamed.

Prang was so close. I knew it was only a matter of moments before he would be after us again. Groaning with pain, Tony tried to stand up. No bones were broken, but he was very, very sore.

"I can't do it," he moaned. "It hurts too much."

"What about Prang?" I reminded him.

The mere mention of Prang's name worked magic on Tony's muscles. Slowly at first, and then with increasing speed, he began to move. By the time Prang had gotten over the surprise and pain of my candle attack, Tony was able to run.

Abandoning all caution, we made our way over the lawn and onto the road. As we ran I could hear Prang approaching. He was just a few yards behind and gaining on us fast. Instead of crossing over the bridge, I got an idea. I headed down the embankment.

Halfway down, Tony slipped on some loose gravel and tumbled to the bottom. As he stood up I saw a shadow move near the water's edge.

"Where shall we hide?" asked Tony.

"We're not going to hide!" I said.

Just then the rat came forward out of the darkness. "You again!" he sputtered, a fishbone dangling from his lips.

Tony backed away slowly. Behind me I heard the faint rustle of leaves. I was sure it was Prang. Without taking my eyes off the rat, I turned my head to one side and caught a strong whiff of Prang. His anger was so intense, I could smell it.

"I told you I'd gnaw your head off!" said the rat, grinding his large ugly teeth. "And I meant it!"

"But I've brought you another friend," I said, trying to sound as pleasant as possible. "And he's right behind me."

"I may be dumb," snarled the rat, "but I'm not stupid enough to fall for that one again."

"No, really!" I said, taking one careful step aside. "Here's my friend now."

As if on cue Prang flung himself out of the darkness. When he saw the enormous rat, a look of total shock flashed across his face. Prang was in no way prepared to deal with such a formidable foe. The rat, on the

HERE'S MY FRIEND NOW.

other hand, seemed delighted. He bared his teeth and spit into Prang's eyes.

My scheme was working. Prang reared up and struck first, but the rat was quick. He jumped straight into the air and pounced on Prang, sinking his teeth in deep.

Stung by the ferocity of his attacker, Prang thrashed about aimlessly, then artfully slung himself around the body of the rat. Three times he coiled himself around the rat's enormous belly. But the rat seemed to have plenty of strength left. As blood was oozing from the wound behind his head, Prang squeezed tighter, but his strength seemed to be ebbing.

At last the two stood locked in a deadly embrace near the water's edge. Without so much as a moment's hesitation I rushed at them and shoved them into the river. Unable to let go of each other, they thrashed about, unwittingly pushing themselves into deeper water. Finally they sank out of sight. A few bubbles appeared, and then, except for the gurgling of the river, all was quiet.

Tony came over to my side, and we both sat down, just plain exhausted.

"You knew the rat was down here all along!" said Tony.

"Yes," I said, feeling proud of myself. "Remember that western we saw on the *Late Night Movie* last winter. The good guy didn't have to fight the bad guys at all. He just got them to fight one another."

"Oh, yeah," exclaimed Tony. "I remember that one

real well. In the last scene when all the bad guys were dead, the good guy said, 'They deserved one another.' "

"That's right," I said, smiling. "Just like Prang and that rat."

But my smug satisfaction was short-lived. As I looked out over the river, I saw the bloated body of the rat floating downstream. Then silently Prang's bloody head emerged from the river, just inches from where we sat. He was still alive and coming toward us! Before he got even halfway out of the water, we were up the embankment and running across the bridge.

(20)

On the other side of the bridge we took to the fields, following the shortcuts Oliver and Josephine had shown me. When we had gone some distance, Tony collapsed, begging me to rest.

"What about Prang?" I said, knowing that was a surefire prod to keep him moving, but this time it didn't work.

"Didn't you see how that rat bit him?" said Tony. "He couldn't be after us anymore."

"I wouldn't be so sure of that," I said. But feeling utterly exhausted myself, I sat down too.

The fog now had dispersed, and the moon, like some giant hurdle-jumper, was bounding over the treetops to the east.

I closed my eyes to rest for just a moment and certainly would have drifted off to sleep if Tony's voice hadn't shaken me.

"PRANG!" he screamed.

"Where? Where?" I stood up, looking all around.

Then I looked down and saw that Tony's eyes were closed. I saw his feet twitching and thought, Poor kid, he must be having a nightmare. I nudged him awake and we set off again.

We trudged through the field and forded a small brook. On the other side of the brook was a cornfield. Here we stopped for a bite to eat, climbing the cornstalks and gnawing the husks open to get at the ripe kernels. After a good meal we felt a lot stronger.

Leaving the cornfield, we came upon a dirt road that I didn't remember having seen before. We were lost. A little farther down the road was a building site for a new house. The ground had been razed clear with a bulldozer and pushed up into huge mounds. I reasoned that if I climbed up on one of those mounds I might be able to get a better idea of the lay of the land and figure out where I had gone wrong.

As we approached the site we passed in front of a cement block wall, the beginnings of a foundation. I was just about to start up one of the dirt mounds when suddenly from behind a pile of boards a long, thin silhouette appeared against the moonlit sky. It was Prang!

We turned and ran along the wall where the path was clear, but it led us only to a dead end—another wall. We were trapped, and before we realized what had happened, Prang was upon us.

"Ssso," he hissed, "your journey ends here."

WHERE?
WHERE?

There was nowhere to run, no chance of escape. I pressed against the wall, knowing the end was near.

As Prang rose up and prepared to strike, blood dripped from his wounds and soaked into the ground beneath. Somehow the air seemed to thicken, and I felt the presence of death. I closed my eyes and wished that I were somewhere else—anywhere else at all.

Then a gush of air almost knocked me over. I opened my eyes just in time to see the outstretched talons of the owl clamp down around Prang's body and lift him into the air. The powerful bird banked to the left and rose into the starry night.

As he flew past the moon we caught one last glimpse of Prang writhing helplessly beneath the great bird.

I stood there watching the now empty sky, and an eerie feeling of calm and peace overcame me. I felt happy to be alive but utterly surprised; I felt no joy in Prang's demise.

(21)

It was early morning when we arrived at Oliver and Josephine's nest. The birds were just beginning to sing, and the sky was a brilliant pink.

As soon as I stuck my head in the passageway, Oliver called out:

"Who's there?"

"It's me. Pearl."

"Oh, Pearl!" cried Josephine, jumping out of bed. "I've been so worried about you."

"Glad to see you back," said Oliver with a sleepy smile. "Did you bring anyone with you?"

"Just my little brother, Tony," I said.

"Oh, come in, come in, both of you," said Josephine.

I could see Tony was feeling shy, so I pushed him ahead and followed him in.

"So this is the young fellow who likes to visit snakes," said Oliver. "Welcome to our home."

Josephine prepared a meal for everyone, and I began to recount the tale of our escape. But I was so tired, when I paused once in the middle of a sentence, I fell fast asleep.

When I awoke hours later, Josephine was busy shelling acorns.

"I guess I dozed off," I said with a yawn.

"You certainly did," said Josephine. "Tony had to finish telling us your story. . . . He's quite a lad, you know . . . reminds me of my youngest, Harold."

I looked around the nest. Neither Oliver nor Tony was present.

"Where is Tony now?" I asked.

"Off with Oliver to gather milkweed for your beds," said Josephine, spitting out a small fragment of shell. "We figured that since only two of you came back, it would be better—for the winter at least—to move in with us. We can just rearrange things a little, and there'll be plenty of room."

"Thank you very much," I said. "But I don't think I'll be staying long."

Josephine stopped her shelling and let her whiskers droop.

"Oh, I had so hoped that you two would stay," she said with a sigh. "Especially Tony. He needs so much to have a good home."

"I know," I replied. "That's why I brought him here. But I have other plans."

Just then Tony tumbled into the nest.

"Oh, Pearl," he exclaimed, "it's so neat here! Oliver showed me a tiny little stream where you can swim in the summer and a hill that's good for sliding when it snows. And we met some real smart birds who have traveled all over the world and Oliver told me a story about a snail he once knew that used to give ladybugs rides on his shell and we got a whole bunch of milk-weed to make beds and later on Oliver is going to show me how to gather food for the winter and all the hiding spots he knows and . . ."

Both Oliver and Josephine were so kind and gentle with Tony. Every night Oliver told him long wonderful stories just like Poppa used to. Josephine took good care of him, too, not just feeding him and keeping him clean, but teaching him everything he would need to know to be a real field mouse.

Tony was having the time of his life, but the days passed slowly for me. Again and again Josephine and Oliver tried to convince me to stay:

"It's a good life out here," said Josephine. "Perhaps you're lonely now, but time, like Father Nature, heals all wounds."

Oliver agreed. "Someday you'll meet a nice field mouse, settle down, and have a family," he added. "Just give it a try. You'll love it."

I had to admit it was a good life out in the field, but something in me felt incomplete. One day I sat down with Tony and told him I just had to leave. I thought he took it rather well.

"You'll come to visit, like Albert promised he would, won't you?" he asked.

"I'll try," I said. "But I may not be able to."

That upset him terribly, and he began to cry.

"Look," I said. "You've got everything you need now. Oliver and Josephine can take care of you much better than Momma and Poppa ever could. But someday you're gonna have to follow your own path, just like I have to follow mine. And there's one thing I always want you to remember. Just because our paths may not be the same doesn't mean that I don't love you."

"Gee, I know that," whimpered Tony. "If it weren't for you, I wouldn't be alive today."

Saying good-bye to Oliver and Josephine was a little easier, but not much. Somehow in a short time they had become a big part of my life.

The night I left, the crescent moon hung in the sky like a thin slice of cheese.

As I set out across the field I looked up and saw a shooting star streak past.

From the field I made my way down the road until I came to Jay's driveway. There was smoke coming from the chimney, and except for the dim glow of Jay's night-light, the house was in darkness.

The window in the cellar was still broken, and it was just as easy to climb in as it was to climb out. I felt my way across the rafters and climbed up through the hole in the bathroom floor. Soon I was climbing the stairs to Jay's room. The door was ajar. I crawled up his blankets, onto the bed, and for a while I just watched him sleeping. Then I walked over and brushed my whiskers against his fingers.

He stirred and, only half awake, looked down at me with sleepy eyes.

"George!" he said. "You've come back!"

Then he scooped me up in his hand and sat up in his bed.

"I knew you'd come back!" he said. "I told Mom that, but she got me another mouse anyway. Her name is Sally. Want to meet her?"

Jay climbed out of bed and lifted me up to the top of his bureau. My cage was in the exact same spot. He opened the door and set me inside.

I went over to my cup and saw another mouse sleeping in it. A wave of jealousy swept over me, and I dearly wished I had stayed with Oliver and Josephine. Then I looked again. It was Wilbur!

I crawled into the cup and nudged him with my nose.

"Move over, Sally!" I said, and lay down beside him.

ABOUT THE AUTHOR AND ILLUSTRATOR

Frank Asch was born in Somerville, New Jersey, and holds a Bachelor of Fine Arts degree from Cooper Union. He is the author and illustrator of many picture books; *Pearl's Promise* marks his debut as a novelist.

Frank Asch lives in Middletown Springs, Vermont.